Making
A Move

Patsy Collins

Contents

1. One Step

I've made up my mind," Livia said.

"And?" Malcolm asked. He put down his drink and took her hand in his.

"I'm going ahead with the kitchen." As she spoke she realised he'd expected an entirely different kind of decision. One about whether she'd allow him to move in, would move into his home, or stay where she was, alone. Livia still wasn't sure about that at all, but getting the kitchen fixed was the first step in sorting out her whole life.

"Ah. Well, I think you've made the right decision."

It seemed he'd taken it as a positive step. She let him. He'd been more than patient and deserved some hope. Besides, it was a positive step. The kitchen was dreadful. When she'd first moved in she couldn't afford to do much. Just hand painted the worst bits and put down cheap lino. She'd put up with it for years. One way and another Livia had put up with a lot. At last she was going to sort herself out.

Livia was divorced. That had hurt. It hurt that they'd split of course but worse was the knowledge they should never have been together. She'd rushed into marriage without thinking it through. She should have got out again quickly, but it had seemed wrong to try to correct one hasty decision by making another. Instead Livia tried to change to suit him.

By the time she was no longer his wife she hadn't felt much like Livia either. Not surprisingly she didn't want to risk that pain again. As a result, after she'd found herself somewhere to live and altered her marital status, where required, on official documents, she'd not wanted to change anything else for some time.

Well, she was going to now. First she'd change the kitchen, then she'd make a decision about her relationship with Malcolm. The kitchen would have to be replaced entirely, she decided. The layout was inconvenient and the appliances all old. Besides, having worked herself up to change, she wasn't going to settle for half measures.

"It'll be very disruptive," Malcolm pointed out. "Why don't you come and live at my place whilst the work is done?"

If he'd said 'stay at my place' rather than 'live' she'd probably have accepted, but the way he phrased it had made it seem like a commitment of some kind. He'd not have meant it that way, Malcolm wasn't the sort to try to push her into anything. She'd not liked to agree, not until she'd made her decision. It would be another step, a bigger one. A step too far?

It was fun planning the new kitchen. Malcolm accompanied her to all the various showrooms, making suggestions and comments in a helpful way. He made it clear the decisions were hers, but she knew what he wanted; her and an easy clean surface. Livia was in complete agreement over the second part. She liked to cook, and wanted to keep her home clean and tidy, but didn't fancy spending hours getting a smear free finish on stainless steel appliances.

Those glass fronted display cabinets looked nice in the showroom, when they contained nothing but a couple of those jars of pickled peppers which nobody ate, or two delicate wine glasses. Fill the cupboards with anything useful though and they'd look cluttered, and cleaning those teeny bits of glass which made up their pretty doors would be the devil of a job.

Livia worried living with Malcolm might become equally awkward and frustrating. Spending a night at his place when they'd been out somewhere was fine. So was having him stay overnight at hers occasionally when that was convenient. They had toothbrushes in each others bathrooms and a change of clothes, but it was a pretence of sharing their lives. It meant no more than those two wineglasses in the display cabinet that'd break in the dishwasher.

Livia chose her new kitchen; a simple traditional design in wood, with a hardwearing, stain resistant work surface. She selected washable paint for the walls, in bright turquoise. Fresh, modern and easy to change if she went off it. She'd get accessories to match, or maybe contrast. Lemon yellow or zesty orange might be fun. She'd wait until it was installed before deciding though. Little details could wait. The big decisions must be made first.

One big decision. Was she going to allow Malcolm into her life, or keep him at arms' length? He'd proposed, but marriage or not wasn't the real question. He'd said she could decide where they lived, but the address wasn't the question. Malcolm himself wasn't even the question. She already knew that, if she decided to share her life with anyone, it would be with him.

Livia had plenty of time to decide, just as she'd had more than enough time to decide if she and her ex husband should divorce. She'd taken too long then and made them both unhappy. There was a danger of that happening again. When the push came it was almost a relief.

"The company I work for are restructuring," Malcolm told her. "I have the choice of moving up to the head office, or accepting a redundancy package."

"Head office? You'd have to move home."

"Yes."

"When do you have to let them know?"

"I have just over two months to make the decision, another four before I leave my current post."

"Do you know what you're going to say?"

"Not yet. It rather depends on you, Livia."

"Me?"

"Yes. It's never been my intention to give you an ultimatum, and I don't mean to now, but my decision will take your wishes into account. If you'd like to move with me, I'll accept the new job. If you prefer to live, with me, in this area then I'll accept redundancy. But if you prefer for us to continue living separately, then I'll take the job and go. It won't make much difference, only in amount of distance you keep me at."

She didn't blame him for the slight edge of bitterness in his voice at the last few words. She knew she'd not been fair to him. That was all very well, but she still didn't know what she wanted, or at least still didn't trust her judgement. She wasn't keen on the thought of him moving away without her, so at least she wasn't faced with more choices than before. Actually there were fewer. Staying as they were indefinitely was no longer an option. As Livia worked from home and had no close relations nearby, where she lived wasn't a concern above personal preference.

So she was back to the one question, did she want to share her life, or did she not?

From the moment Dean the kitchen fitter parked his van outside her house, she was temporarily sharing her life with a man. It was oddly intimate having him there. Livia constantly had to step over him or squeeze round him. It wasn't romantic or anything like that. Maybe it could be in some situations, but not with her and Dean. He was half her age and newly married. It was kind of nice though, having someone about. Working from home could be lonely. When she stopped for a coffee there was someone to talk to. She could open a packet of biscuits knowing she wouldn't eat them all herself. If either of them went to the shop they enquired if they could get something for the other. He wasn't Malcolm though. Dean didn't get her jokes, or know which article in the paper was likely to interest her. Dean wanted to please her, but that was so she'd pay, would recommend him to others, and because he had professional pride. It wasn't because her happiness was important for his.

Dean saw parts of her life no one else had for a long time. Her dirty laundry when she made her last use of the old washing machine. The way she looked carefully at the post before opening it. He didn't tell her not to be daft and just open it. Of course Dean wouldn't. He was too busy double-checking the measurements of the work surface and unlikely anyway to criticise his client's little peculiarities.

Livia was like Dean in one way; they both double-checked everything. Dean did cut though, once he was ready. Livia might too eventually, but she was still double-checking and second guessing. Malcolm might cut soon. If so it would be along the line she'd drawn.

Would Malcolm laugh at her studying the post, turning the envelope over in her hand? Maybe he would and she wouldn't mind. There was one thing he wouldn't do; rip it open before she got to see it. Just as he hadn't told her which cupboard doors to pick, but had gone with her to take another look. Had understood her need to be really sure.

"That's it then. The water's going off and the sink's coming out," Dean told her.

"How long will I be without water?"

"In the whole house, an hour or so now and the same again, maybe a bit longer, in a few days when I fit the new one. But it'll be a good five days of washing up in the bathroom I'm afraid."

Livia had been warned and knew that afterwards she'd not be able to walk through the kitchen and therefore get into the garden for two days when the new floor was laid. That's why Malcolm had suggested that she live with him, temporarily. It had been a very sensible suggestion and one she should have accepted. Would in fact accept. It would be a step, not a step too far, hopefully not one in the wrong direction.

"I think perhaps I'll go and stay with my friend for a week or so," she told Dean.

"No problem. I've got your mobile number in case I need to ask you anything."

Livia smiled. She always gave Dean an answer. It was time to give Malcolm his. She'd put off her decision for fear it would be the wrong one, but letting Malcolm move away without her answer would be a much bigger mistake.

She rang him to say she'd like to stay with him while the kitchen was finished.

"A sensible decision, I think," Malcolm said.

"Yes. That's the second one I've made recently and I have a feeling it's going to be third time lucky. We'll talk about that tonight."

"I look forward to it. Shall I collect you after work? And perhaps pick up a bottle of wine?"

"Good idea. Make it something with bubbles in."

She checked her watch. She had plenty of time to go shopping before she need pack. Livia intended to buy two wine glasses. Pretty, impractical wine glasses, so she and Malcolm could toast the first step of their new life together.

2. For The High Jump

"I suppose it's too late to change my mind?" Helen was only half joking. She'd asked her husband James to drive her mainly because she was worried her nerves would be so bad she might not be safe behind the wheel, but also to make sure she didn't chicken out.

"If you really aren't happy you don't have to do it, but yes you have left it a bit late."

"I'm not happy, but people are relying on me."

Helen was making a charity parachute jump to raise money to help children like her little nephew. People said he was brave, the way he battled his problems and was so cheerful, but he didn't really have a choice. She did.

"If I go ahead with this, the extra money will help children like Luke have choices. The chance perhaps to jump out of a plane one day if that's what they want."

James squeezed her hand as they walked across the car park. "You'll be fine, love. I'd have tried to talk you out of it otherwise."

That's true, he would. When she first said she was going to do this, he'd told her how amazed and impressed he was.

"I'll need a lot of help from you," she warned him. "You won't be so proud when you see how scared I am."

"I will. You could have joined your sister on the charity run instead, couldn't you?"

Helen was starting to wish she had. She tried to make a joke about keeping her feet on the ground and not worrying about airtime, but her words came out in a stuttering jumble. They always did when she was nervous. Once in school she'd been asked to read a poem to her whole year group and it had come out like something written by Edward Lear.

"Take a deep breathe and speak slowly," James said.

Helen did as he suggested. "Running … is … boring."

"And you're not bored now, are you?"

She wasn't. Neither was she truly terrified, she realised once she had her breathing back under control. That was thanks to the support of James and Ted. James had brought her here, where her ordeal would take place, for a kind of dry run the previous day.

He and Ted smiled reassuringly as she'd sat for a moment in the seat she'd use, tried on the equipment for size and was shown the red light which would signal her leap into the unknown. No, she was being dramatic there. There'd be no leaping and although it was a first for her, she knew what would happen and she'd have Ted with her.

He was experienced and he'd understood that this was a big deal for her. "Don't worry, Helen. I'll guide you through the whole process. All you really have to do is hang in there."

"I can do that."

"Great, then I'll see you tomorrow. Just remember why you're doing this and everything will be fine."

Helen spoke on the local radio. The DJ had introduced her and explained about the charity and what Helen intended to do in order to raise money.

"Why would you want to jump out of a perfectly good aircraft?" he'd joked.

Helen had a moment of panic. "Well … er …"

The DJ chattered on, covering her hesitation and making it easy for her to give very brief answers. Whilst 'Jump' by Van Halen was playing a local celebrity rang to say he'd double however much Helen raised. She was speechless. It was generous, but put even more pressure on her to do well.

"You are doing this because of your nephew, I understand," the DJ prompted.

"That's right."

"Tell me about him."

"He needs constant medical treatments and to always be close to a hospital, but that could all change." Once she thought about Luke, rather than what she was doing, Helen was less nervous. She spoke persuasively about the charity and encouraged listeners to donate whatever they could.

Soon the interview was over. The red light went out, Helen removed the audio equipment from her head and hugged James who'd been waiting just outside the tiny studio.

"That wasn't so bad was it?" Ted asked.

Helen grinned at the DJ. "Terrifying. Ever since school I've found it difficult to speak to more than one person at a time. Today tens of thousands of people, many of them strangers, were listening to me! It was worth it though and now I can look forward to the jump. That's going to be great fun!"

3. Simple By Design

Joanna unrolled her work before the committee. They crowded around the poster she'd designed for the forthcoming Norton-on-Sea 'Special Day'. She'd created a scene which represented the town. It showed its proximity to a good beach, hinted at its history, showed the range of shops already in place, plus suggested many of the attractions which would be available on the day. Over a clear blue sky were the words 'Come for a special day out at Norton-on-Sea'. The date and times of the event were printed close to the bottom, followed by the event's website address. It had been a lot to cram in, but the committee had insisted all those things were to feature.

What they'd asked for was almost impossible and Joanna had been under a great deal of stress as she worked, but she'd managed it.

"Lovely," they said, or "very nice," or "so pretty." Behind every compliment Joanna could hear a silent 'but'. She should have known. Lately it seemed nothing she did was right for anyone.

It was only a moment before the silent criticisms were said aloud.

"It's maybe just a little busy, dear," one lady said.

Joanna once again explained that including everything they'd wanted made for a complicated and confusing image.

11

She reminded them she'd suggested they have a water colour sketch showing the view down the High Street and out to sea, with the date and website address written in the sky.

"But then it wouldn't show the manor house. That's a historically significant building and quite a draw for tourists," a gentleman said.

As the other committee members began voicing their opinions, Joanna wished she could just walk out, but some of these people were friends of her dad so it would be his reputation as well as hers that she damaged.

"The hotel must be included. The owner is our biggest sponsor."

"Leaving out the church would be wrong as this whole thing was the minister's idea."

"I've included everything you asked me to," Joanna pointed out as calmly as she could.

"You have, but with the writing it's hard to see everything. Couldn't you just add the date to the top and not have that bottom bit?"

"There aren't any people. I think there should be people enjoying themselves."

Suggestions were made of various local personalities who could be added, and that children be included.

"No youths though. We don't want them."

"I'd like more flowers. So many residents have made a real effort with their gardens."

"A list of the major events should be on it too, I think."

"And perhaps directions?"

Eventually Joanna said, "If I can just clarify what you want … it's a simpler design that incorporates everything I have already, plus a lot of extra features. You want children, but no youths. You want less writing, but for there to be more words?"

"That's it exactly. When will you have it ready for our approval?"

"I'll be in touch," Joanna muttered. She packed up and left before she could say anything she might regret.

In the car park she took a few deep breaths so she could concentrate on her driving rather than the frustrations of her life. Once she was calm, she headed home. Although she managed to drive safely, she couldn't keep her mind free of worry.

Just before she'd been briefed to create the poster, she'd had a huge row with Larry. He'd gone away with work for two weeks and although they weren't quite at the not speaking stage, they'd not been in contact much. He'd not phoned or answered her calls. All she'd had were a few texts saying he'd arrived safely and the mobile phone signal was weak. That was probably true, but if they'd not rowed she was sure he'd have found a way to contact her more frequently.

Usually if she'd shown signs of doing anything as idiotic as being briefed by a committee Larry would have talked her out of it. He didn't even know about the mess over the Norton-on-Sea poster. She missed talking things over with him. She just plain missed him.

She didn't blame him for being upset. What man wouldn't be after his fiancée said she didn't want to get married after all?

Joanna did want to be married to Larry, she just couldn't face the wedding. The trouble had started from the moment they'd tentatively announced an approximate date.

"But that's during Wimbledon fortnight," her mother had said after making a note in her diary.

"I don't see why that matters, Mum."

"Your cousin Millie might be playing."

"I still don't see why that matters." Cousin Millie was actually more like third cousin six times removed. They never so much as exchanged Christmas cards.

"Having her there might add a touch of class."

"Class?"

"Well I suppose you'll have to invite your father and it wouldn't surprise me if he dragged that woman along."

"Chana won't be dragged along, she'll be invited. You'll expect us to invite your husband, I presume?"

"Naturally he'll be there as he'll be giving you away."

"No. Dad will."

A beep of the horn from the car behind her reminded Joanna she was supposed to be travelling home, not stopped at a junction lost in thought with her hands gripping the wheel and foot stamped on the brake. She waved in apology and moved forward.

Making progress with the wedding plans hadn't been so simple. Although he didn't say so, Joanna's father must surely hope the service would be held in Norton-on-Sea church. Her mother would want it held near her home town over a hundred miles away. Larry's parents were dropping hints about top hats, marquees and a string quartet. Joanna's best friend, a redhead, had pleaded that pink be excluded from the bridesmaid dresses, despite it being the first choice of the bride's dark-haired sister.

Larry had suggested they have a simple, inexpensive wedding rather than start married life in debt. Joanna had yelled that, as it wasn't possible to please everyone, they'd just not bother at all. That would save money, arguments and a bitter divorce like the one her mother had put her father through.

Remembering that scene, Joanna's hands were once again frozen on the wheel and her foot jammed right down on the brake. Fortunately she'd arrived home by then. She slammed the car door, locked it and went inside.

She was greeted by evidence the last week had been spent on artwork rather than housework. A waste of time that had been! Joanna shoved a load of washing in the machine, collected abandoned crockery and washed it, then emptied the overflowing bin. With the house looking a little less abandoned, she filled the kettle and dropped two slices of bread into the toaster.

A minute later she smelled burning. As she remembered a crust had come off the slice she'd put in the previous day, and must be wedged in the toaster, the smoke alarm went off. Joanna frantically flapped a tea towel underneath it. The clamour of the alarm was joined by the insistent beeping sound which told her the washing machine had finished its cycle. She couldn't stop both of them at once. Trying to do so was no more possible than taking everyone's wishes into account over the wedding, or the publicity poster.

Once peace was restored, Joanna made herself a mug of tea. At least the kettle simply did its job and shut up. Everyone was happy with that and never expected or wanted more. Joanna rather wished she were a kettle.

In a way she used to be. When Larry first proposed, she'd accepted but said she wanted to concentrate on her business first. "Can we live together for a year or two first?"

"Sure, if you like," he'd said.

They'd not asked anyone else's opinion. No one had objected, or made things difficult. She and Larry had been very happy. When she first began creating commercial artwork she insisted on working with a single client and to a clear brief. Her work had been highly praised. Then had come all the hassle of organising a wedding and the mess over the poster. No more.

Joanna sent a text to Larry. 'So sorry. Love you. Want to marry you and be a kettle. X X X'.

A very short while later she got a reply. 'Love you too. Kettle??? Home tonight xox'.

As she waited she started to think. Of all the opinions she'd received about the wedding, only one really mattered; Larry's. Well, and hers too of course, but she'd been so caught up in what everyone else wanted she'd hardly given it a thought.

Larry was right, she decided. Getting into debt in order to please other people, who'd likely not be satisfied anyway, was just silly. What she really wanted was to be Larry's wife. She'd like rings on their fingers, a photo on the mantlepiece and memories of a happy day, but even those things weren't vital. The only thing which truly mattered was that she share her life with Larry. When he came home, they set to work planning their wedding and sorting out the mess over the poster.

The committee almost gave in to Joanna's insistence that she liaise with just one of them. They said the hotel owner and church minister could make the decision.

"Sounds reasonable," Larry agreed when she told him. "Those two probably know something about weddings, too."

Three months later all their friends and family arrived at Norton-on-Sea. First there were special prayers in the church to bless the forthcoming wedding, for those who wished to attend. Everyone did, even Joanna's mother, though she did manage things so as not to sit next to Chana.

The wedding itself was an informal affair, held in a marquee in the hotel grounds. As it had been erected especially for the town's 'Special Day' rather than their own, Joanna and Larry weren't charged extra for that. Joanna's mum and stepdad booked a two night stay, so as not to have to travel on the day.

The four bridesmaids all wore dresses in the same style, but in each girl's choice of colour. Joanna's father gave her away. Her stepfather was delighted to be asked to give the only reading; a fun poem he composed especially. Later the best man read out messages, including one from Cousin Millie at Wimbledon who'd got through to the quarter finals in the mixed doubles competition.

Joanna's mother only made one snide comment about Chana. "I see she didn't wear a proper hat, just one of those fascinator things."

"That's right. She told me she didn't want to eclipse the mother of the bride, not that she could of course."

"She said that? Perhaps I misjudged her."

Half an hour later the photographer caught a candid shot of the two women giggling together at Joanna's dad trying to dance with the youngest bridesmaid who held him firmly around the knees.

A string quartet, along with other members of the school music group, played during the reception. They were rehearsing for the town event, on the following day. The committee it seemed had relented about youths, as well as the poster design.

As Joanna and Larry were leaving, she saw her work on display in the hotel lobby. The last photo in their wedding album was of the newlyweds posed either side of a poster showing Norton-on-Sea's High Street and the view down to the sea. Written in the sky were the words 'Come to Norton-on-Sea' for a special day.

"That's exactly what we've done," Larry said.

4. Trying Everything

"I've tried everything," Ceri said. She sipped unsweetened herbal tea, trying to look like she was enjoying it.

"Everything but the obvious course of action," Leanne corrected. She took another forkful of gooey chocolate cheesecake. "You know what I…"

"I have, honestly!" Ceri butted in before Leanne started another lecture. "I've cut out sugar and white bread." It was torture, as was watching her so called friend eat the most delicious looking treat with obvious pleasure, but she'd stuck to her diet for weeks.

"And is it making you happier?" Leanne asked. "Is it making Nick any nicer to …"

Ceri ignored the first question and talked over the second. "I have loads of vegetables and whole grains."

"That's great if it makes you happy, but it isn't, is it?"

Ceri could barely bring herself to admit it, but she shook her head.

"Then don't do it. You're a lovely person, a great friend, you're fun, pretty…"

"Yeah, yeah."

"You are! There's only one thing wrong and that's…"

"That I keep interrupting you?"

Leanne laughed. "Something like that."

As they were leaving, a young man, with a small child holding onto one hand, tugged at the door. It didn't budge, so he pulled harder, his attention all the while on the boy.

Ceri pulled the door towards her.

"Thanks. Oh!" He tapped the 'push' sign as he went in.

"I've been doing that, haven't I?" Ceri said. "That's what you've been trying to say, that I'm approaching this all wrong?"

"Pretty much."

"Don't worry. I know what I've got to do."

"Oh?" Leanne asked.

"Exercise. That's the answer."

"That's not what…"

"Gotta go. Call you later!"

Ceri smiled all the way home. Nick would be so pleased she'd seen sense at last.

He was less enthusiastic than she'd hoped when she told him about her plans to burn off the fat, especially when she asked if he'd like to come with her.

"Walking? That won't do much good."

"Not just a stroll; power walking."

"Waste of time and it looks silly."

He didn't like how she looked when she stayed still, so it wasn't surprising he wouldn't like the look of her striding out pumping her arms.

"I'll come circuit training with you then," she suggested.

"What? You haven't got the right gear and you'll get all red and sweaty and embarrass me."

Walking it was then.

Ceri changed into comfortable jeans and trainers and headed out. Without meaning to, she power walked to the shop. Maybe Leanne was right that a really strict diet wasn't the way to solve her problem. A tiny bar of chocolate might stop the cravings.

"I've tried everything," said the person in front of Ceri in the queue. "I just can't shift this sore throat."

The lady had cough sweets, lemons and painkillers.

"Have you tried local honey? I've heard that helps," Ceri suggested.

"I have, yes. On its own, with lemon, with whisky. I'm going to try them all together next."

"There's a herb my gran used to use. Sage maybe?"

"That's the one. Tried it and gargling with antiseptic. I've slept with the windows open, the windows closed, tried scarves and those things you heat in the microwave. Nothing works."

"That's six pounds forty-seven please," the assistant said.

"You'd better give me sixty superkings too. There's rain forecast tomorrow and one thing I do know is it won't do my sore throat any good coming out in that."

"Cigarettes?" Ceri asked.

The woman seemed unable to hear her. Of course she could have heard if she wanted to but, just like Ceri, she was choosing not to. No doubt others had told her smoking was ruining her health, just as Leanne had told Ceri what was ruining her happiness.

She called her friend. "This exercise thing, I was wondering if you'd help?"

"If you really think it'll make you happy."

"It might. I'm going to warm up with energetic packing of my stuff ..."

"And cool down at my place with a glass of wine and a takeaway?"

"Yeah. I think that workout will work out." Until Nick criticised her weight she'd been quite happy with her size 14 curves, in fact she'd been happy about everything until he'd started to undermine her confidence. She'd tried everything else to put things right, now at last she was taking the obvious course of action and leaving him.

5. So Long, Sue

Tony really missed Sue once she was gone. He'd taken her for granted a bit, he supposed. Even considered her a nag. He believed he'd actually said that to her once. Hah! Believed! He knew full well he did. Tony had decided it would be nice to go out for a proper roast in a quiet country pub one Sunday. You probably know the sort of thing, low beams, wood fire, roast beef and Yorkshire puddings, half a pint of the local bitter. It would be a nice change for them both, he thought, instead of being stuck inside. Poor old Sue used to spend a lot of time inside, waiting. Well, she couldn't get out on her own, could she? Tony had to go out without her sometimes.

Just before they were due to go that Sunday she wanted some water. She had a little problem that meant she needed water fairly frequently. Not really her fault, Tony knew, but it did get irritating.

"In a minute," he said. He wanted to programme the SatNav first but she wouldn't shut up about the water. He gave her some but was none too careful about it. Splashed some on her as a matter of fact.

"Sorry, Sue," he said as he dabbed it off with clean tissues. "But can't we just for once have a trip out without your nagging?"

She was as good as gold the whole day after that, which left Tony feeling guilty.

Well, she might not have been a total nag he admitted to himself, but she did remind him constantly whenever there was anything he wasn't doing right or that she considered she needed. It'd start first thing in the morning, even before he'd left for work and continue until she was settled down for the night. Sometimes it was just a visual clue, like a red glint in her eye to warn him of impending trouble if he didn't act quickly. Other times it was an audible sign, anything from a quiet rumbling to a high pitched whining. That last just couldn't be ignored.

To be fair, not all that nagging was self-centred. She worried about Tony's health and comfort at least as much as her own. She never let him drive a yard without his seatbelt on for example. And whenever he returned to her embrace she made him feel warm and secure.

She needed a lot of attention though, did Sue. Sometimes Tony had to cajole her to get any kind of response. Then once he had got her going he had to be careful how he handled her. Not that he minded that. A bit of spirit was a good thing in Tony's opinion.

He daren't neglect Sue or he'd pay dearly. Actually he literally paid dearly whether he neglected her or not. Lots of money was spent on her each year. Tony knew better than to forget any of her anniversaries. There'd have been a world of trouble if he did.

Tony had no intention to dwell on the negatives though, not once she was gone. He'd try instead to remember the good times. There had been a lot of good times. Holidays, especially their first trip abroad. Tony was nervous about the ferry, worrying how he'd get her up those steep ramps but he needn't have worried. Sue managed beautifully.

She was brilliant with the kids too. Tony sometimes looked after his older brother's kids on a Saturday. The kids loved Sue. They scrambled all over her, pushed her places she didn't really want to go, and played daft games with her. Once or twice they were even sick on her! She never complained, not once. The moment after Tony had her cleaned up it was as if it had never happened.

Tony took Sue everywhere with him. Well, everywhere he could. He did almost everything for her, only calling in the professionals when he really had to and he was sure that had made them closer. He felt completely lost without her.

He'd been right to move on though. Get a replacement for Sue. It sounded heartless, but what was a man to do?

Tony had taken his mate Jim's advice. "Just get yourself a new younger model, mate. That old one was a heap. Warning lights coming on every five seconds and costing a fortune to run and get through the MOT. You'll be much better off with a new car."

6. The Shop Girl's Daughter

"*Plus un timbre pour l'Angleterre s'il vous plaît*," Paulette said, placing her postcard and souvenirs on the counter. One stamp would be enough; she'd be back home soon. She held out a handful of francs and centimes so he could take the required amount. Although she hadn't forgotten the few useful phrases she'd learned in school, she still wasn't able to properly communicate. She'd found French people spoke their language faster, and with stronger accents, than Miss Bruton had.

"*Merci*," she said when he'd taken his money and handed her a bag containing her purchases.

The man complimented her on something. Paulette's language skills weren't strong enough to know if it was the wisdom of her choices, her attempts at communication or perhaps even her new miniskirt. She smiled at him anyway.

The song on his radio changed to The Beatles' latest hit. "*Oh, tres bon*," she said.

The shopkeeper shrugged. "*Comme ce comme* ça."

Paulette was delighted; he might not share her taste, but she'd exchanged opinions with the man. "*Au revoir*," she said.

He said the same in reply.

French wasn't the only language she'd attempted. When she'd gone ashore in Barcelona she'd said, "*Por favor, dos sellos para Inglaterra.*" From there she'd written to both her dad and her former teacher. She'd done the same at Cadiz too, although she'd had to ask for the stamps in English at several ports.

Paulette found a tempting café and used another of her useful phrases, "*Un thé doux s'il vous plaît.*"

Sipping her sweet tea, Paulette stuck the stamp on a card showing a pretty landscape. It seemed odd not to see the Queen's head. Of course the French wouldn't have that but they didn't have a silhouette of Charles de Gaulle either. It was such differences which made foreign travel so interesting to Paulette. The lovely weather and landmarks were good too, but she barely had time to appreciate them. Instead of rushing round trying to see everything in a few hours, Paulette preferred to take a stroll, buy a few small trinkets and her postcards, then have a drink and soak up the atmosphere.

She wrote to Miss Bruton. She said how much she was enjoying the trip and reported her French lessons had come in useful in Belle Ile, Monte Carlo and now Nice. Would the teacher be more surprised Paulette remembered the phrases she'd been taught or that she'd visited places she could use them?

Just for once Paulette wasn't writing to Dad. He'd be waiting at the docks when she disembarked the cruise ship, so she'd give him all her news then. Paulette had travelled so far and she'd come a long way from the council house in which she'd been born during the war. Who'd ever have guessed she'd end up seeing the world by luxury cruise ship?

She'd had a mixed start in life. If her dad hadn't had a reserved occupation as a dock worker she'd never have been born at all. His job meant a few extras in the way of food made it onto their table without the need for ration stamps. He knew some foreign words too and a lot of interesting stories.

Mum had been so much fun. She'd taught Paulette to do the jitterbug, the words to all the songs in the hit parade, how to make butterfly cakes and sew appliqué decorations to clothes and household linen. Then, when Paulette was ten, she'd got ill and died.

For a time it looked as though Paulette would have to leave her dad and live with other relations, but thankfully she'd got a place as a border at Meadow School. It was the best school for miles and very expensive, but they took a few bright girls on scholarships. Paulette wasn't particularly bright, but for some reason was offered a place.

All the teachers treated her fairly although one, Miss Bruton, had been extremely demanding. She gave Paulette extra assignments and expected a standard of work which Paulette simply wasn't capable of, no matter how hard she tried.

"You must do better, child! Otherwise you'll end up nothing more than a miserable shop girl."

Paulette's new friends said she might well be a shop girl, but would never be as miserable as Miss Bruton, whom they nicknamed Brutal Bruton.

"You can add up well enough to give the right change and I bet you'd be great at finding people exactly what they wanted," her friend Angie said. Others agreed.

"I'll be your best customer."

"No, I will and I'll time my shopping trips so we can have lunch together."

Being a shop girl sounded to Paulette like it might be rather fun. She asked her dad what he thought when she went home for the weekend.

"Nothing wrong with being a shop girl. Your mother was before we wed. That's how we met. Though with the schooling you're getting maybe you could do something different."

"Maybe, Dad. Girls can do pretty much any job they want these days, but I'm not sure I want to carry on studying for a career. Working in a shop might be the best thing for me."

"Reckon that'd suit you just right, love and you'd always have work. Everyone needs shops don't they? Harrods is a shop and I bet your snooty teacher wouldn't look down her nose at people as worked there."

Paulette wasn't so sure about that.

"If man ever makes it to the moon like they're planning they'll probably put shops up there too," Dad said.

"I'd apply to work there! Be fun to work somewhere more exciting than the High Street."

Paulette's next run in with Miss Bruton came at the start of the following term. She wanted everyone to write about their holidays. "Use all your senses. I want to feel the sun on my skin, smell the exotic flowers, taste the foreign food," she said as she paced round the classroom. Then she'd stopped right in front of Paulette. "If you didn't go abroad that doesn't matter. Tell me what you tasted, saw or felt even if it's the stickiness from the pick and mix counter in Woolworths."

A few girls sniggered, but Paulette wasn't sure if it was because they found it amusing her dad couldn't afford to go anywhere by aeroplane or because Brutal Bruton had put her foot in it.

Sure enough everyone but Paulette wrote about foreign travel. Paulette loved listening to their reports; to her it made her friends seem as glamorous as Omar Sharif, Elizabeth Taylor and Paul McCartney. Paulette wrote about her week in Clacton. There was no point trying to make that sound glamorous, so Paulette hadn't tried. Instead she described what it felt like to get so much sand in her costume it sagged down well below where it should have been when she got out the sea. She said how odd she'd looked after sitting to read under the pier and getting just one sunburned arm. For the sense of smell she wrote about riding on a donkey which kept stopping abruptly, causing Paulette to slip forward and get a face full of grey hair. Taste was covered by the time she'd spread strawberry jam on unfamiliar garlic bread. When Paulette read out her work she also gave a good impression of the Punch and Judy show.

Paulette's cheerful nature and sense of humour soon made her popular with everyone except Brutal Bruton. The teacher continued to push Paulette hard and be disappointed with the rather average grades the scholarship pupil attained. 'Could do better' was her usual comment on end of term reports.

"I do my best, Dad. Honest I do," she said.

"I know you do, love. The other teachers say so too. Very polite it says you are here and this one says you're always pleasant and cheerful and all but one say you work hard. Seems that Miss Bruton don't like you, though I can't see why."

Paulette couldn't understand it either. As far as she knew she'd never done anything to upset the woman. It was worrying because by then Miss Bruton was deputy headmistress and would be one of the people who wrote the references Paulette would need to get a job.

Every summer Meadow School held a fête at the end of term. Paulette's last term was no exception and she was looking forward to it. The girls all took turns running stalls and, as one of the senior girls, she could take her pick.

"The book stall, please," she'd said. One of the perks involved was that she could look through the donations early in the day and use her pocket money to buy any she particularly liked. Paulette had already seen a beautifully illustrated atlas.

She'd decided to buy it so she could look up all the places her friends had visited and dream of one day seeing them for herself.

Once that book was safely in her possession, Paulette devoted her attention to helping her customers make selections. It was fun to see someone recognise an old favourite from their childhood, or tempt people to look at something they would never usually have considered.

After her hour working on the stall Paulette was free to look round the fête herself. She'd given up almost all her own money for the book, but as her dad had to work he'd given her enough to buy tea and a slice of cake. She took that to where some classmates were looking at photographs pinned up in the hall. They were of teachers, taken when they were children and there was a prize for whoever correctly identified the most.

It was hard to be sure about a lot of them. Some were of babies in Christening gowns so even telling if they were boys or girls was difficult.

"I think that one might be Mr Williams," Angie said. "Looks like his ears."

Paulette agreed.

"There's one that should be easy, because the girl is quite a bit older, but I still don't know."

Paulette looked at the photo, which was of two girls. One had an arrow pointed towards her, so as to identify her as a teacher. Paulette immediately recognised the other person. She gasped. "That's my Mum!"

"Are you sure?"

Paulette was very sure. There were only a few photos of her mum in the house. The only one that didn't also have her dad in it was of Mum and a friend, both aged about ten. The picture in the school sport's hall was, like the one at home, faded and hard to make out, but she recognised the pattern of cherries on the girls' dresses. Mum told her she'd made it herself and her friend had made one too from a huge tablecloth. Paulette explained that to Angie.

"The teacher must have been a friend of you mum, then."

"I suppose so, but none of them have ever said."

Angie went to fetch tea and cake, leaving Paulette trying to remember what else Mum had said about her friend.

Mum's words came back to her. "She went to a different school after that was taken and I didn't see much of her. Perhaps I should have kept in touch. We used to have a good laugh."

Maybe it was the headmistress? She'd always been really kind to Paulette. That would explain why Paulette had been offered the scholarship, but any of the other teachers could have put in a good word for her. Or maybe the teacher in the photo didn't realise Paulette was the daughter of her old friend? It had been a long time ago and Mum had a different surname to Paulette's then.

Paulette became aware that someone was standing at her side, also looking at the photo; Miss Bruton.

"Do you know who this is, Miss?"

"I do, child. I do." Miss Bruton gave a quick lopsided smile and walked away.

Did she mean she really knew, or that she'd guessed?

Angie came back then, with her own tea and a jam tart for Paulette. "What did Brutal Bruton want with you? Giving you an extra job?"

Paulette explained what had happened. "The way she'd said it and smiled made it seem she did know and that perhaps there was something funny about the answer."

"It's old Richards the caretaker?" Angie suggested.

Paulette laughed. "Doubt it. Look, I was thinking, the only way she'd know for sure was if it was her."

"Can't be."

They looked again.

"It could be, I suppose. Her hair's different, but the nose and eyes are a bit like Brutal's."

"I guess she's about the same age Mum would have been too."

"Nah, she can't have been friends with your mum," Angie said. "She'd have been nicer to you for one thing."

Before Paulette could reply, Miss Bruton asked to have a word with her.

"Have you worked it out now?" she asked once they were alone.

"I think so, Miss."

"I was your mother's friend once," the teacher said. She looked sad.

"Was it you who got me this scholarship then, Miss?"

"I did put your name forward, yes."

Paulette tried to thank her but was cut off.

"Please don't thank me, I feel bad enough as it is."

"But why, Miss?"

"We both tried for a scholarship here. I got it and as you know, became a teacher. My life is comfortable and happy. Your mother was not so lucky. We stayed in contact for a while, though infrequently because we were at different schools. Your poor mother didn't gain any qualifications as far as I know."

"I don't think so, Miss. She got a job though, straight out of school."

"Yes, shop work wasn't it?"

Paulette nodded. "Yes, but she loved it and it's where she met my dad."

"She was happy?"

"She was, Miss. Ever so happy. Always singing and laughing and dancing."

"I see."

"I think I do too, Miss. You've always been on at me to do well because you wanted me to have the chances Mum never got."

"Yes. I thought if I helped her daughter do well then it would make up for taking her chance away from her."

"You didn't take anything away from Mum, Miss. There is something you can do for me though… I'll need good references if I'm to get a job."

"You'll have them from all the teachers I'm sure, Paulette."

Miss Bruton was right. Although Paulette left school with few qualifications she had glowing references from all her teachers, Miss Bruton included.

When her dad told her about a job he thought would suit her she'd applied right away and got it. She was delighted as it meant she'd get to see all those interesting places her friends had written about and it would give her the chance to prove to Miss Bruton that a girl could be happy, even if she worked in a shop. That had been true enough for Mum working down the High Street, but it was even more true for Paulette, serving in the gift shop on a cruise ship.

7. First Impressions

I love the beach early in the morning. Slipping off my sandals, I allow the water to splash my feet, washing away my footprints as though I'd never been there. Sometimes even to wash away my sadness.

I'm usually alone except for gulls and occasional joggers who leave me in peace. Since the fire I don't like being noticed. Just as a damaged wire once sparked and destroyed my home, a stranger's gasp of surprise, when they first saw my face, destroyed my confidence.

Like many young women I was hoping for romance. I was unlikely to find it partly, I admit, because I refused to try.

A month or so ago a man walked, as I did, barefoot at the water's edge. A silky-haired Labrador bounded excitedly around him. I moved away despite my sister's advice.

Suzy had said I didn't give people a chance.

"I don't want to settle for anything less than perfect and I don't want someone who thinks I'm second best either," I told her.

"Of course not, Amy. I just mean you should try to see beyond people's initial reactions."

Suzy was right; but she didn't know how hard it was to speak to someone while they stared at your marked face. At least she'd stopped saying it didn't look as bad as I thought.

I'm being unfair. Suzy looked after me brilliantly whilst I recovered from the shock of the fire. She'd given me a room, for as long as I wanted, in her hotel and a job in the office. Now she wanted to help me find love, or at least friendship.

I tried again to explain. "I don't want people looking at me and seeing a scarred girl, I want them to see a girl who just happens to have scars."

"That's how I see you. It's how a lot of people would see you once they knew you; if you ever gave them that chance."

"I'm not sure I can."

"Why not practise on holidaymakers? Just say 'hello'. You needn't see them again."

I glanced round for a change of subject and saw a man in dark glasses, with a golden Labrador in a harness.

"I could try with him. He wouldn't mind the scars."

"Philip? Yes, he'd be a good person to talk to."

I'd promised Suzy I'd go out a bit more, try talking to people. Since then I'd walked along the beach each morning. Other than joggers, I'd only seen one lady. She stopped to chat about the weather. She stood quite close, so must have noticed the scars, but didn't react. A rare check of my reflection confirmed they were still there, but I began to think they might be more important to me than to other people.

It was no longer determination to hide that made me avoid the man and his dog; it was habit. A habit I intended to break. He was almost level when I smiled at him. He ignored me.

I stared after him as he walked along the water's edge. Just as happened with me, the waves washed away his footprints as though he'd never been there. He had though and for the first time I saw in him what others really saw in me. Suzy was right, they saw a girl who had scars – and who rebuffed most friendly gestures. I wouldn't do that anymore.

Next day, he was there again. I walked closer and saw he was the man Suzy called Philip. His dog bounded over. I stroked her. Philip approached and said, "Good morning."

I'd been too quick to judge, he'd simply not seen my smile the previous day.

"Good morning," I replied. Not original, but a start.

We met every morning after that. I told him about my job and how Suzy was teaching me to be useful in the hotel. He told me about training Lucille. Philip told her to sit, lie down and stay which she did impeccably. She could do much more, he assured me.

I saw him walking on other occasions and we usually exchanged a few words. About a month after our first meeting, Phillip invited me for a meal.

"I can't! I'd never have spoken to you if I'd known you lived here. I thought you were a holidaymaker."

"I don't understand." As he spoke, he touched my arm, just above the scar on my elbow. I flinched away.

"Sorry," we both said together. Embarrassed I rushed back to Suzy.

I told her I'd messed things up with the first friend I'd made since the fire.

"If he's really your friend, he'll forgive you," my wise sister pointed out.

So now, I'm waiting for Philip on the beach and enjoying the remains of the sunrise reflected in the sea. It's beautiful that light, possibly even when it shines on me.

I call the moment Phillip's in sight.

He seems pleased. "I thought I'd upset you, Amy."

"It was my fault. It was because of this." I lift his hand to my face.

He strokes the rough scar and his expression doesn't change. "So, you have a scar. What's the problem?"

Put like that I realise there isn't one.

I notice his dog isn't with him. "Where's Lucille?"

"She's gone to her new owner. I thought you knew I'm a guide dog trainer?"

Suzy was right, I must stop judging people on first impressions and learn to look below the surface.

8. The End Of Lady Grimshaw

The invitation to the school reunion came as a surprise. I was surprised there would be a reunion at all and even more surprised that I was included on the guest list. I'd had fewer friends than most and hadn't kept in touch with anyone. St Margaret's was a wonderful old building and the school had offered excellent teaching and a wonderful opportunity to local girls. Even so, for most of us, our days there probably weren't the happiest of our lives.

When I noticed we were to reply to Elaine Robertson, the mystery of why I'd been invited was solved. She'd been the secretary. For all I knew she still was. She, like most of the staff, had seemed quite old but in reality were probably only in their forties; the decade I and my former classmates were fast approaching. I guessed Mrs Robertson had access to school records. Although I'd moved away, I was once again back in my childhood home, living with my mother who'd had me late in life and been alone since I reached my teens.

"You should go, love," Mum said.

I'd not been back home long and didn't really know anyone. Some of those who'd gone to St Margaret's probably still lived in the area Mum reasoned and imagined I'd easily resume former friendships. But then she didn't know how things were at St Margaret's and that as a result I had no friendships to resume. She'd had more than enough troubles of her own back then and I'd not wanted to add to them.

Was Mum right? Should I go? It was at least a chance to lay a ghost; that of Lady Grimshaw. She'd been no lady at all, not in any sense of the term, but the school bully. She'd made everyone's life miserable, mine included.

I didn't accept nor decline the invitation right away. Instead I decided to do a little online research before making a decision. St Margaret's itself seemed the obvious place to start. I discovered the financial slump meant the money left to fund it was no longer enough to provide free places for all girls, as it had in my day, but that a few pupils were still accepted on a scholarship basis.

Whilst on the school's website I discovered a link to the 'old girls' forum. I signed up using CC as my online name, but didn't join the discussions. Almost everyone else used either their initials, a nickname, or just their first name. I could hardly identify any of my former classmates. It was as though they were now a different group of people, which of course they were. Many were wives and mothers, some had responsible jobs, one was back at St Margaret's as a teacher. I was different too. There was no husband or glittering career to brag about, but neither was I ashamed of the person I'd become.

There was plenty of talk about the reunion on the forum. Pupils from other years were invited too, but my contemporaries were the most active in those discussions. I suppose everyone thought, much as I did, that becoming forty was a time to take stock. Still looking forward, but looking back too. We'd all made mistakes we could learn from, but there were successes too. We'd all have plenty to talk about when we met. Indeed many had already started.

Perhaps unsurprisingly, a lot of chat was about Lady Grimshaw. Many of the girls recalled how miserable she'd made them. I was glad to see that, although the memories were still a little bitter, most girls had moved on.

"I retreated into a dreamworld to escape all the horribleness which was the reality of my life back then. Now I write children's stories for a living." That was from Anya, not a name I recognised as belonging to any of my classmates, but the mystery was explained when she revealed herself as novelist Anya Angus.

"It's my pseudonym, but also my real name now. I'm a different person, so it seemed reasonable to have a new name."

I thought people would ask who she used to be. I'd have asked, had I joined in the conversation at all, but instead everyone posted comments about her books. Those with children the right age were especially interested. It seemed the reunion might be good for her already rather impressive sales. Maybe it could help others too? Particularly those still suffering from Lady Grimshaw's taunts. I knew that kind of thing could carry on into later life. At my first job I'd been terribly bullied by our supervisor. Fortunately it wasn't just me she picked on. The staff all got together and told her it wasn't acceptable. She'd crumbled immediately. It's often said bullies are insecure underneath and it was true in her case. After we confronted her she'd stepped down for a while, received further training on management techniques and started afresh in a new department. Last I heard she was doing OK.

Thinking that example would help with the Lady Grimshaw issue I plucked up my courage and made a post in the forum, saying that since leaving St Margaret's I'd learned a little about bullying. I described how my colleagues and I had together stopped a bully in her tracks. It got a reaction, just not the one I'd hoped for.

"Yeah, let's gang up on her. Give her a taste of her own medicine," Louise wrote.

Distant taunts of, "Lousey Louise," echoed in my memory. If this was the same girl I quite understood why she was so keen on revenge. Lady Grimshaw had forced her head into the toilet to wash away the nits she claimed Louise had passed onto her. Although they probably suspected the truth, no one had been brave enough to point out the infestation had occurred the other way round, at least not to Lady Grimshaw's face they didn't.

Plenty of others agreed with Louise's strategy. That's not what I'd intended. At work it had all been calm and reasonable, but a private party would be a different matter especially as alcohol would be involved. I hadn't thought it through properly.

"No, that'd make us no better than her," Polly said.

"That's true," I'd quickly typed. "Haven't we all had enough of that kind of behaviour?"

Polly, or Roly Poly, as she'd been known back then, wasn't someone I'd liked as she'd once got me into quite a bit of trouble with the headmistress. I was going to put that behind me though. I know she had her reasons at the time.

I knew too that Lady Grimshaw had reasons for her behaviour. Not ones which excused how she'd behaved exactly, but they went some way to explaining it. She'd been brought up to believe she was better than the other girls. Her dad was the boss of nearly all their dads. She lived in a house he owned, not a council terrace. Her clothes were new, not hand-me-downs. That was all common knowledge and how she'd got the nickname Lady. There had no doubt been a little jealousy, and she was a tiny bit of a snob, but she'd not really been disliked for our first year or so at St Margaret's.

Then her dad got caught fiddling his accounts. He'd made a right mess of it and as a result some men lost their jobs. Mr Grimshaw had been sent to prison. Expecting to be hated or ridiculed, his daughter had attacked first.

That's the thing, there's always something behind people's actions. At work we learned the supervisor who'd bullied us had a bully for a father. She was just carrying on the behaviour she'd learned as a child. I wondered how many of my bullied classmates were now unkind to their colleagues or treated their children too harshly. None I hoped, but I wasn't confident about that. I thought if Lady Grimshaw was confronted in a calm, reasonable manner and apologised, maybe even gave an explanation for her actions, perhaps the cycle could be broken.

Soon the 'old girls' forum talk was all about who would be attending. Although she said she'd try, I guessed Roly Poly Polly wouldn't. She'd been ten stone aged ten, eleven stone aged eleven, twelve stone … You get the idea. Aged thirty-nine she could be any size.

Mrs Robertson (I still couldn't think of the former secretary as Elaine, despite her using that name on the forum) said not many people had confirmed one way or the other. I was one of them, so sent back a yes. Soon Mrs Robertson reported that nearly everyone had replied to say yes – including Lady Grimshaw.

A plan was hatched; we'd all get there early and prepare ourselves to confront her.

"Who is going to tell her?" Louise asked. "How about you, CC? It was your idea."

"Sorry, I just can't," I typed and suggested Polly.

"I'm still not absolutely sure I can make it," she said.

Eventually Louise said she'd do it, as long as everyone else was right there backing her up.

On the day, I dressed and made-up carefully and was reasonably pleased with the results. I'd not been an attractive child but I'd improved as I matured. Now with subtle make-up and a hairstyle which suited me, rather than the frizzy permed 'big hair' and harshly outlined eyes, plus nice clothes rather than the detested and ill-fitting school uniform, I wasn't recognisable as the unhappy child I'd been.

There was a flurry of greetings as I arrived. I didn't immediately recognise anyone and what with people giving either their forum identities, school nicknames, or introducing themselves by whatever variation they currently used, I wasn't too sure who most of them were. Elaine Robertson was the obvious exception, she'd hardly changed and one or two others looked familiar. No one seemed quite sure who I was. Some were sure and called me by the wrong name. I laughed as I'd made mistakes too.

Some of my classmates looked better than me, some not so good. Some were doing better financially, some had children, some had jobs and others boasted of careers. It was as it should be. Everyone had something to be proud of.

Louise made herself known and revealed her plan for confronting Lady Grimshaw. "I've decided not to say much, in case I mess it up, and you'll all be with me, won't you?"

She received plenty of assurances, then the door banged and a new arrival swept in.

"That must be her!" Louise said. "Lady Grimshaw."

The woman certainly looked as though she thought she was someone. Great figure, skin, hair. Huge smile.

We all surrounded her and Louise edged her way to the front. "Although it's a bit late, I … We, want to tell you that we think … The thing is, bullying is quite unacceptable."

The woman's smile faltered just a fraction, then beamed brightly again. "Don't worry girls, I put it behind me a long time ago. Part of my weight problem was due to a thyroid problem. Once that was diagnosed I felt more confident and started to eat better and exercise. Now, well …" She gave a pretty little laugh, put her hands on her hips and wiggled them.

"You're Roly … er, Polly," I gasped as her words sank in.

"Roly Poly Polly, yes I was. Not any more though." Then after a moment, "Who did you think I was?"

"Lady Grimshaw," Louise said.

"She's not coming, is she? Wouldn't have thought she'd have the nerve."

"That's what we thought. In fact CC here said a lot of bullies are cowards underneath."

Polly glanced around at us all. "Well, it seems she was right. Lady Grimshaw isn't here."

"Actually she is," I said. "CC stands for Caroline Chloe. I could have added the G which stands for Grimshaw."

"You can't be!" Anya said.

"But … but you're nice," Louise added.

Once they'd recovered from the shock, I gave them a partial explanation and full and heartfelt apology. Their forgiveness was the last stage in exorcising Lady Grimshaw. Knowing she doesn't haunt the others means I too am now free of her ghost.

9. Mysterious Lights

"Seen any more alien landings lately?" Dawn's great niece asked.

Dawn shook her head. "I've already explained they're not aliens."

"You've explained nothing," Sindy protested. "You're totally dotty and imagined doing that as well as seeing the lights."

Dawn grinned. Although Sindy was generally very shy, with her great aunt she was a cheeky little madam, which made her good company and fun to tease. They'd always had that sort of relationship. For her fourteenth birthday Dawn had given Sindy a huge book on mathematical theory. When the disappointed girl was coaxed into opening it, she'd discovered Dawn had painstakingly cut a large hole in every page and slotted a comprehensive make-up kit into the gap.

Once Sindy had asked Dawn what Queen Victoria was like. "We're learning about her at school and I thought it would be good to get first hand information."

"Awful child! If you've learned anything at all you'll know I'm far, far too young to have met her."

"No good saying that when the evidence is right there," she gestured to the shelf holding Dawn's photograph albums.

"Show me."

Sindy had done something clever on a computer and produced photographs which appeared to have Queen Victoria alongside Dawn at school, in her garden, and at the beach.

Dawn chuckled. "It seems you're right. I suppose I'd forgotten all about spending time with her after meeting the king."

"Which one? Edward? George?"

"No, silly. Not *a* king, *The King* – Elvis. Not that I knew him for long, but you can imagine the impact he had."

"Seriously, you met Elvis Presley?"

"Got you!" Dawn had said just a little smugly.

Now, several years later, she told Sindy, "I don't know why you're imagining aliens are responsible for something which has a perfectly rational explanation."

"That's not what you said when you first saw them. You said we might never solve the mystery."

"Well, *we* haven't. *I* have. Now I want to solve the mystery of why a lovely young girl like you is always round at her allegedly dotty aunty's house, not out with a charming young man."

"Because as soon as one is nice to me I turn into a gibbering wreck. Guess that's why I like you so much. You're never nice to me."

"Don't change the subject. You liked the boy selling ice creams, didn't you?"

"Yes."

"Then go back and see him."

"I wouldn't know what to say. Unless it's pointing out how dotty you are, I'm no good at talking."

"In that case I won't tell you what the lights are. You can work it out yourself. Should be easy enough as you have the advantage of not being dotty."

"I do, but I don't think that makes up for your advantage."

"Which is?" Dawn asked.

"Being the only one of us who's actually seen them."

"That's true."

The very first few times Dawn saw the lights they'd hardly registered at all. Her sightings had been fuzzy glimpses of red from the bathroom, which could have been almost anything. Then one evening she'd stayed up a little later than usual, watching television, and saw them more clearly through the lounge window.

They moved rapidly, and apparently haphazardly, within a limited area – a bit like the way Sindy had waved sparklers when Dawn took her to firework displays, although on a bigger scale. There were two equally sized lights, but they didn't move in unison as car's lights would. Besides they were too small and not bright enough for that. After less than a minute they came together, paused, and then drifted out of sight.

She'd seen them quite regularly since, always around the same time. They appeared in the distance, getting gradually closer and closer, as though drifting or being blown down the road. Once roughly opposite Dawn's home they'd pause, then suddenly separate to perform intricate patterns. Whether they went into the churchyard, Dawn wasn't sure. At times one or other would momentarily disappear, which might indicate they moved behind a gravestone or the railings, but Dawn sometimes noticed the same thing on their arrival and departure. The strange display lasted anything up to ten minutes. Afterwards the lights came together again and then left, just as slowly and steadily as they'd come.

Dawn wasn't frightened of them. They were quiet and although where they stopped was very near Dawn's home it wasn't directly outside.

As near as she could tell it was usually outside the semi-detached properties three and four doors down, but the position varied. If they were attempting to give a message of some kind it didn't appear to be directed at anyone in particular.

They didn't come very late – Dawn went to bed quite early. It wasn't unusual for people to walk, drive or cycle past in the evenings, so if they were caused by anything very strange someone would have noticed. If it was children messing about she'd surely have heard them, or heard about any damage they'd caused.

The only way in which they caused Dawn any concern was the worry she was imagining them, and therefore actually as dotty as her beloved great niece claimed.

One night just after the lights had gone, Dawn heard her neighbour putting out his bin. The following day she called round and said, "I thought I saw lights over there in the churchyard last night. Have you ever noticed anything?"

"Can't say I have. I wouldn't worry though, it's probably car taillights showing through from Church Road."

"Ah, yes. Thank you." Dawn knew it wasn't, but was still reassured. He'd said taillights, which were red. Dawn guessed he had seen them, but like she had the first time, dismissed them as unimportant.

The obvious thing would be for Dawn go out one evening and take a closer look, but she didn't want to. She enjoyed the mystery. Guessing Sindy would too, Dawn had told her great niece when she next visited.

"Did I mention my lights?"

"Are you trying to pass off your grey hair as highlights?"

"No, I just say they're the result of being related to you! These are real shining lights, but not really mine, even though I think I'm the only one who's noticed them signalling."

Sindy leant forward in her seat. "Go on."

Dawn had described the lights in detail, possibly exaggerating their spooky nature somewhat.

"And you've no idea what they are?"

"I've had lots of ideas. Could it be one of those drone things?"

"You think the Russians are spying on you?" Sindy asked.

"No, as I keep saying, I'm not dotty. I meant the sort people take pictures with. Could they do that at night?"

"No idea. There were people flying things on the common as I drove by. Not sure if it was drones or model planes, but we could go and have a look, see if they move the same way."

"Good idea. There's an ice cream place down there which serves interesting flavours, so I'll treat you to one of those."

Sindy grinned. "Pity it's unusually warm today, or we could have hot ones. You do remember that?"

"I do." They'd once spent an hour looking for fossils on a windy beach before Dawn had suggested ice cream, 'to warm us up'. The hot chocolate and whipped cream, served in a stemmed glass and decorated with a flake, had looked exactly like an ice cream sundae and six year old Sindy had been impressed.

It was harder to catch her out as she grew up, but Dawn still tried. She'd befriended the young serving lad in the ice cream stand partly with that in mind. She enjoyed the look on Sindy's face when she'd asked him for a Brussel's sprout and pea ice cream.

Even better was when he'd replied, "Sure thing," and put two scoops of different green ice cream into her cone. "Any gravy on that?"

"Of course!"

"Same for you?" the lad asked Sindy.

"No thanks." A blushing Sindy spent a long time looking at the menu. Easily long enough to work out Dawn had been given mint and pistachio flavours with chocolate sauce. "I'll play it safe and go for a classic gin and tonic."

"Good choice." He heaped a huge amount of ice cream onto Sindy's cone. "There you go. A double G&T. Do you like the real thing too?"

"Um, yes, I…"

"Would you… " he started to say, but Sindy had grabbed both cones and dashed away, leaving Dawn to hurry after her.

Sindy tasted her ice cream. "Oh my days, it really does taste like gin! Yours isn't really sprout flavoured, is it?"

So it wasn't the menu which had held the girl's interest for so long, Dawn thought. That was interesting. "As you weren't brave enough to order it, you won't know unless we go back another time and get one."

"I don't think I can. I was such a dork."

"No you weren't, Sindy love. But don't worry about that, let's check out the flying machines."

The two of them soon decided neither model planes nor drones accounted for the lights Dawn had seen. They were as unlikely to have been carried whilst switched on as they were to be flown at night.

"Bicycles?" Sindy suggested.

"Wouldn't the lights be white?"

"I was thinking of red reflectors being lit up by the street lamp."

"That would be the right kind of light. I don't think you could ride bikes around in the churchyard like that, but we could go and look."

"I'd forgotten that bit of ground was a churchyard. Maybe they're ghosts?"

The bicycle theory was discounted – there really wasn't room for them to be manoeuvred at such high speeds even in the daylight. Ghosts visiting a graveyard didn't seem likely either.

"Must be aliens then," Sindy had decided.

A few days later Dawn attended a local history talk about in the library. The timing meant that as she returned home she'd seen the lights at close quarters. She'd immediately understood what they were. After that Dawn quite often went down to be amongst the lights, and the causes for them. She hadn't immediately told Sindy though. That was partly because she didn't want Sindy thinking she was silly for not realising sooner. Partly because it was fun listening to her ever wilder theories, but mostly because she was waiting for the right moment.

Now the time had come.

"Are you doing anything this evening?" Dawn asked.

"Nothing special."

"Which is a real shame for a young thing like you. Still that won't stop me taking advantage. How about we get a takeaway to share? Afterwards you can watch the lights and see if you can work out what they are."

After chow mein and pancake rolls, the pair of them went upstairs and looked out the open bathroom window. They had only a few minutes to wait until the red lights came into view.

"They look as though they're being carried," Sindy said. "Infra red torches, perhaps?"

"Keep watching."

Sindy did. When the lights began to dart about and leap into the air she admitted understanding why Dawn had been puzzled. "They do look mysterious, but I think I know what they are."

"Come on then clever clogs. Let's go and see if you're right."

When they reached the churchyard gate it was easy to see two dogs which each had a small light on their collar, so they could be seen in the dark.

"I was right," Sindy said.

"Which makes you nearly as clever as me."

"What have you … oh!"

The dog's owner had noticed the two of them. "Hello again," said the lad from the ice cream stand.

"Sindy, you've already met Gareth, and these are Pluto and Moon. Gareth, this is my great niece Sindy. She does like gin and tonic and the pub on the corner is dog friendly."

"How about it, Sindy? Will you come for a drink?"

"I… um… "

"Please," Gareth coaxed. "Only you can tell me if your aunt is really as dotty as she seems."

"You're very clever indeed, Aunty," Sindy whispered, then took a step towards Gareth. "She really is."

Dawn watched them walk away until all that was visible were two red lights drifting steadily into the distance.

10. A Stranger's Kindness

Laura was sorting laundry when she found an artist's business card. Odd. She'd not been to an exhibition or gallery in ages. The name Charles Harrison meant nothing. Unless he was the stranger who'd been so kind?

Just over a week ago, Laura's youngest had moved out. He'd found a job that was perfect except for being so far away.

"I'll phone often, Mum!" he promised.

She knew he would, just like her other kids did, but she wasn't going to sit at home waiting.

It had been lovely on the coast – invigorating. A stiff breeze, the tang of salt, great light. She watched families with dogs playing in the surf, saw couples hand in hand, even the birds flocked together. Laura experienced a sudden feeling of loneliness and sank onto a bench.

"Are you OK?" a man had asked.

Laura started to say she was fine, but couldn't find the words.

"It's OK, you don't have to pretend," he said. "I'll just sit here. Ignore me if you like, or walk away, or you can talk."

She'd done none of those things. Instead she'd felt silent tears slide down her cheeks.

He hadn't touched her or spoken, but somehow it was comforting to have him there. After a little while he'd handed her a pack of tissues.

"Thank you." Then, after accepting one, added, "I'm so sorry, I never cry."

"Sometimes we need to."

He'd been right. Other than being embarrassed, she'd felt better straight away.

She remembered now that he'd given her his card, 'In case you feel like talking'. At the time she'd felt silly and hurried away. Now she felt bad about that. It had taken a great deal of kindness, and a little courage too, to approach her as he had. She should thank him, let him know he'd done the right thing.

Laura sent a grateful text.

Charles replied a few hours later. 'So nice to hear from you. I often walk along that bit of coast for a couple of hours. I'll be by the ice cream kiosk most Wednesdays at two. If you ever want to join me for a stroll I'll be delighted to see you, but won't be offended if not.'

She didn't go that week but did go the next.

Laura hadn't really taken in what he'd looked like, but when she saw a man facing out to sea she was certain he was Charles. He was of medium height and slim. She'd have guessed he was fit even without knowing his habit of long walks.

A couple asked him to take their photo. She recognized his voice as he replied. Deep, but gentle too – a little like the purr of her cat Cocoa. When she purred Laura found the sound soothing. Charles's hair must have once been the same rich brown as Cocoa's fur, but was now liberally sprinkled with silver. She liked that he'd not tried to disguise it. Everything about him seemed genuine.

Charles directed the young couple to stand in a certain place. Laura moved so she could see why and realised it was where the light would be on their faces and the background was of the sea without any distracting rubbish bins. Of course an artist would notice things like that. He gave clear, confident instructions without seeming bossy.

"Pretend you like each other," he joked.

The couple moved closer together. "I don't just like her, I love her!" the boy said.

From the girl's reaction it was his first public declaration. Clearly she felt the same way.

The camera clicked. Charles didn't just have a knack of persuading people to open up, he also had great timing.

He turned, allowing Laura to see his pleasant face, which looked as though a smile was never far away. As if proving her right, Charles grinned at Laura. He raised a hand in acknowledgement, but didn't come closer. If she'd wanted to she could have waved and then walked away.

When Laura took a few steps in his direction Charles immediately came forward. "It's a lovely day for a walk. Would you care to join me?" he said.

There was no pressure, and she had no hesitation in accepting.

As they walked they chatted easily. About the view, the people they saw, the weather. There was nothing to it but easy companionship. Not yet.

With her heart beating a little faster, Laura suggested, "Perhaps we could walk together regularly?"

"I'd like that very much," Charles said. He grinned again and Laura knew her own face was a picture of happiness.

11. A Walk Along The Canal

Every day, regardless of the weather, I walk along the canal path. It's not too far; twenty minutes from my front door to the High Street. Just enough to make me feel I've done some exercise. The path is straight and level so even in winter, when it gets dark so early, it's no trouble to negotiate. It runs along the edge of a woodland for a few hundred yards, but for the most part passes houses and a school playing field. At one point there's almost a tunnel where the railway bridge goes over it. All that, added to the boats going to and fro, assorted wildlife, fishermen and dog walkers means there's always something interesting to see.

There are plenty of reasons to make the journey. I withdraw my pension from my account at the Post Office. Our little town has an excellent library, a butcher, baker and greengrocer. Even a place where you can buy candles and other pretty bits and pieces. There are several charity shops, more estate agents than we can possibly need and two tea shops. These are good, but I don't use them often. It doesn't seem right on my own.

I didn't realise at first that I was lonely. Why would I? I've never needed lots of people round me and when I have wanted a friendly acquaintance I've never had trouble achieving that. My aunt inadvertently taught me the trick when I was about nine and I overheard her and Mum talking.

"I'm just so lonely," Mum said.

"I'll put the kettle on," my aunt soothed. "A cup of tea always helps."

I went down to join them. I missed Dad too, we used to talk about everything together. Besides I thought there might be cake on offer. There often was when the teapot got filled.

Peter started coming round for tea soon after that. He'd been a friend of Dad's and eventually became my stepfather. Mum and I moved into his house before I went away to boarding school. Mum and Peter said it would be a good opportunity but made clear the choice was mine. They took me to have a look and meet the other girls. Everyone was friendly.

The school wasn't so far from home that Mum and my stepfather couldn't visit. They came most Sundays and Peter took us out for a nice tea. He encouraged me to bring friends which helped make me popular.

Muriel became my special friend for two terms. We chatted endlessly, sometimes even in lessons! We shared books and toys and of course always had our meals together. Muriel never ate even half of hers, so I finished it up. That didn't stop the teachers noticing she was sick, but all they or anyone else could do was watch helplessly as she faded away. Now things would be different, but this was fifty years ago.

Of course I mourned Muriel and missed her company, but I wanted to stay on at the boarding school and soon made new friends. It was easy enough. All I had to do was approach one of the new girls and ask if she'd like to come with me to the café in town to get a milkshake. That was the young girl's equivalent of a nice cup of tea, though I don't suppose I thought of it like that. I chose girls who had fathers in the military or who wouldn't be staying long for another reason. They were the most likely to be lonely and so accept my offer of friendship.

Since then I've had plenty of friends, but never really got very close to anyone. My choice and I've been perfectly happy. I like meeting people, especially those different from me. There was plenty of opportunity for that at work. We often had people on exchange visits from similar organisations or interns gaining a few month's work experience. An offer to show them how the coffee machine worked was enough to have us on friendly terms. That was as close to real friendship as I wanted.

I was invited to, and attended, various social functions but never stayed long. I didn't get involved in dinner parties and that kind of thing. Don't get me wrong, I wasn't a loner. Often I'd accompany someone on a day out, for a meal, to the cinema or the theatre. I could sit up late chatting to a friend over a bottle of wine and frequently offered a shoulder to cry on when needed. I enjoyed people's company, but never the same person too often or for too long.

There were family events too. Weddings were my favourite, I like to see people happy even if their route to it isn't the same as mine. Birthdays and christenings always felt a little awkward, but I knew what to do at funerals. I made tea and let people talk. I went back after the fuss had died down, made more tea and invited the bereaved person to share happy memories. Several people have told me that helped with their grief. I'm glad to have played a role in easing the pain which I've spared myself.

The main reason I didn't realise I was lonely as soon as I retired was that I wasn't, not then. You see I moved straight after. For some time I'd liked the idea of living somewhere less crowded, perhaps even having a bit of garden but there wasn't anywhere suitable I could both afford and commute from. Without the tie of my job, or any other ties come to that, I could live where I liked. Getting ready for the move and settling in kept me busy for a while.

I enjoyed getting to know the area. As I've said the town has everything I need and is a pleasant walk away. The neighbours were something of a disappointment. Nothing wrong with them really, just they're too much like me. Or too like I had been up until then; polite but distant.

So you see, while I was busy filling my days with walks along the canal, I'd become lonely without even noticing. Perhaps I should have realised when I decided to climb up into the loft? I didn't need to put anything up there or have any concerns about the water tank, I was just looking for something to do and it was somewhere I'd yet to explore. I found a couple of boxes. 'Books' was marked on one and 'coats etc' on the other.

I took my second walk along the canal that day, to ask the estate agents for the contact details of my home's previous owners. Of course a phone call to the agents would have done as well, or I could have written to the couple using the address they'd given me for forwarding mail. That I decided to visit the estate agent in person and then speak to the people directly was probably due to my unacknowledged urge to communicate with someone else.

It was as I was walking back with the phone number scrawled onto a compliment slip, that I first saw the homeless person. I didn't pay much attention that first time.

"Oh yes, they must be ours," the woman I'd bought my house from said after I'd described the boxes.

"You're welcome to collect them any time," I said.

"Thanks but we downsized when we moved. As we've managed without whatever is in them up to now we obviously don't need it. If there's anything you'd like, do please have it and perhaps you'd be kind enough to take everything else into a charity shop?"

"Yes, if that's what you want." I brushed aside the offer to pay for any costs I might incur, assuring her there weren't likely to be any.

I sorted through the books, putting aside a few to read myself before taking them, via the canal path, into the charity shops. I inspected the clothes too. There was a scruffy waterproof jacket, two of those fleece things and several scarves and woolly hats. The only thing which appealed to me was a coat in a gorgeous burnt orange colour. It was too big for me and the kind which is all puffed up like a quilt, so looked even bigger than it was. Giving a donation to the charity shop would be as good as taking it in, but I knew I wouldn't wear it often, if ever. Better for it to go to someone who'd make use of it.

Taking the books and other items to town, a few at a time, provided me with plenty of exercise over the next few days. The cold didn't bother me. I'd dressed accordingly and the canal path was fairly sheltered for most of the way and there was warmth in the charity shop. Some supplied by electric heaters and some by Barbara who worked behind the till a couple of days a week.

"These should sell well," she'd remarked when I brought in the first bundle of books.

For some reason instead of just nodding, I told her how I'd come by them.

"So, you're new to the area. I've lived here half my life, so if you've any questions just ask."

I didn't ask, but she supplied information on each visit regardless. She extracted some too; never asking anything too personal, but still persuading me to talk for a time each day. It made a pleasant change and I reminded myself I could take the donations to the other charity shop, or deliver them on her days off, if I decided I'd had enough of her conversation.

Nothing Barbara did spoiled my walks. It was the sight of the homeless person, who seemed to have taken up residence under the bridge, which did that. I didn't feel threatened; for one thing they were on the opposite side of the canal and never called out or anything. I felt some pity. Maybe they'd brought it on themselves, quite possibly not, but whatever the reason behind their situation it must be hard living rough in the winter. I was annoyed with them though for bringing harsh reality into my comfortable life.

It was when I realised I had no one to mention the person to that I saw how lonely I'd become. I could have told someone, but that would have taken the nature of reporting them to an authority, which I assumed would bring them added trouble. There was nothing to justify my taking such a step, but neither did I feel able to ignore the situation completely. I wished I had a friend to confide in, perhaps come with me to offer food and blankets. Part of me wanted to do that myself, but I knew nothing about the person or what they might do. The charity shop where Barbara worked and to which I'd taken all the books and clothes helped homeless people. I made a donation too. It was something but not, I felt, enough.

As I delivered the last of the books, I noticed the orange coat which had only been put on display two days previously was already gone.

"You sold that quickly," I said to Barbara.

She, as usual, was all too ready to chat, and it occurred to me she was exactly the kind of person I'd once have avoided. You see she was a regular at the library and although steering clear of that one charity shop would have been no hardship, I did like to sit for an hour or so in the library. It was a good place to rest before walking back home and as well as borrowing books I liked to browse the magazines and papers. Letting Barbara think I would welcome a friend would ensure I rarely got to do that in peace again.

"Um, not exactly …" she said. "I hope you don't mind but I gave it to a homeless girl. Poor kid has been living under the railway bridge this last week."

"Oh."

"Maybe I shouldn't have given it to her, but aren't we here to help people like her?"

By 'we' I assumed she meant the charity shop, but I was pleased to have played a small part by delivering the coat and so nodded my head.

"Tell the truth I didn't know what to do for the best when I first saw her. I walk right by her as I come into town and I thought she could have been drunk or crazy or something. She never did anything though. Actually I didn't even know she was a girl until last night. It started sleeting about four-thirty you might remember?"

I nodded again.

"When I left I took the coat with me. I paid mind, I didn't steal it."

"Of course."

"I didn't get too close to the girl, just said 'here you are' and chucked it at her. But when I heard her thank me and realised she was just a kid, I went back. I offered to get her some help but she begged me not to tell anyone about her. Suppose I shouldn't have told you, but I live on my own and I don't know what to do."

"It's OK, I won't tell anyone," I promised. Well, there wasn't anyone I could tell, was there?

Another customer came in then and I was able to slip away. I went over to the library but didn't read. Instead I sat and thought. There seemed to be three options. First I could do absolutely nothing except keep my promise. I need never go back to the charity shop and I imagined that Barbara might be embarrassed over her indiscretion and avoid me. That was slightly cowardly, but it occurred to me that most of my human interactions since losing my dear schoolfriend Muriel had been slightly cowardly.

Secondly I could go to the police, or social services or something like that. It wasn't what either of the others wanted, but I didn't owe them anything, did I? But I didn't know anything about the girl and didn't want to make her situation any worse.

The third option meant getting involved. Talking to both Barbara and the girl and working out what to do for the best. It meant making friends with them. The girl, with luck, would soon move on somewhere better, but Barbara wouldn't. Helping meant making friends with someone who wasn't about to move away, with someone who might come to mean more to me than any friend I'd had since I was ten years old.

Making friends is something I know how to do, even if just recently I've not put the knowledge to use. I went back to the charity shop.

"Barbara," I said. "Are you doing anything in your lunch break?"

"I usually go to the tea shop on the corner."

"Perfect. Would you mind if I joined you?"

"I'd be delighted." She looked it too.

"And may I bring a young guest?"

"The homeless girl you mean?"

I nodded at her once more.

"OK, if you think she'll come."

So I'm walking now along the opposite side of the canal to the path I usually take. I'll offer to buy the girl some soup or a sandwich and a cup of tea and I'll offer Barbara my friendship. I hope they'll both say yes. After that, I'm not sure what will happen, but I imagine I'll keep walking this path every day and I don't think I'm going to be so lonely.

12. Coach's Plan

Judy and I had been working together for a couple of months by the time we both attended the same three day training course. I'd seen her about, and liked what I saw, but we hadn't really spoken much. The course was in a hotel and we had the choice of staying there, all expenses paid, or travelling daily. As Judy and I opted to travel, and lived fairly near each other, it made sense to car share.

We chatted about all kinds of things on the journeys, including her son. She confided she was having trouble coping with him. "His behaviour is the reason I couldn't stay in the hotel."

I decided against telling her my reason was a flame haired nurse who'd finally agreed to a date and instead asked, "How old is he?"

"Fourteen."

"A difficult age."

"I hope it's just a bit of teenage rebellion, made worse by losing his dad eighteen months ago. He's a good kid underneath, but sometimes it's hard to see that."

"I wonder if rugby might help?" She already knew I was a volunteer coach but until then I hadn't mentioned it was to local teenagers. "I've seen sport make a huge difference to some troubled kids."

"I don't know."

"Maybe we could talk about it over a drink?" I suggested.

"I'd like that, but Ryan definitely wouldn't."

Even so, she did agree to have lunch with me in the coffee shop when we were both back at work.

"I haven't mentioned anything to Ryan," she told me.

"Oh?"

"When his dad died suddenly, he took it badly… as is natural. Then he seemed to be coming to terms with it and we were quite close until I went on a date a few months ago. My sister came round so he wasn't alone, but she had to call me to come home after less than an hour."

"It's OK, you don't have to tell me."

"I think I'd better if… well… He doesn't know, but his dad and I hadn't been getting on and would likely have split up before long. Ryan idolised him when he was alive and now in his memory he's perfect. He was angry at me for betraying his dad as he saw it, and angry at Jake for trying to win my affection. He said some horrible things when we came back."

"It sounds as though he's insecure and worried he'll lose you too."

"Probably. Doesn't help me much though."

After a few more, very pleasant, lunchtime chats, we came up with a plan. Judy's sister would suggest the rugby coaching to Ryan and if he seemed keen, Judy would let him talk her round.

"Isn't that a bit underhand?" she'd asked. She's not as sneaky as I can be if it seems warranted.

"You don't have to lie to him, just express the doubts you had when I first mentioned it."

"All right. I suppose that will let him make up his own mind far more than if I tried to push him into it."

It wasn't long until I was seeing Judy two evenings a week – when she dropped Ryan off and picked him up from practise. She was so formally polite that anyone watching, Ryan included, would surely think she heartily disliked me. Judy would have liked to stay with her son, but I didn't encourage that. An audience at matches seems to help the boys perform. Having yummy mummies around during training is a distraction none of us need.

Ryan didn't cause me any particular problems. I hadn't expected him to. All the lads seemed to like and respect me as a coach, but perhaps not surprisingly those without a dad looked to me to partly fulfil that role. There are similarities; I do care about them and not just on the field. I'm interested in their general health, diet, how they get on with each other and in the rest of their lives. If they don't eat or sleep well they can't play well. If they get grounded at home, detention from school or in trouble with the police they can't attend training or matches. Not that I'm totally focussed on rugby. I like the boys and want them to have happy, well rounded lives. I want the same for myself too and that includes occasional dates with an attractive woman.

I also enjoy the kudos of 'discovering' talented young players. Usually they're spotted at school, but a few don't develop their skills or enthusiasm until it's a bit late for that. Local junior leagues give them a chance to play and big clubs sometimes take an interest. Our local professional team is no exception and we had a game against their junior squad coming up.

I'd not expected Ryan to be particularly good at the sport, but he surprised me. He was a natural and, once he saw a little of his own talent, worked hard. When he concentrated and managed to channel his energy and emotion the right way, he was a fine player. I can't and won't single out one boy as a favourite, but I'll admit to being delighted with his progress. Every one of my lads wanted to play in the forthcoming 'big' game. Ryan was almost certain to make the cut, but I didn't hint to him, or any of them, who I was considering. Instead I made it clear they had a few more weeks to impress me. Clever, albeit sneaky, trick of mine to make sure no one was late for practise!

Judy hugged me. "Thank you for all you're doing. Ryan's a much nicer person to be around and his teachers have reported a marked improvement in both his behaviour and grades."

"Have you said anything to him?"

"He only communicates in grunts, but that's progress from alternately yelling or giving me the silent treatment as he did before. I don't want to push it."

I told Ryan how proud I was of him, both because it was what he needed to hear and because it was true. He confided in me sometimes; all the boys did. I allowed them to get things off their chests and if appropriate steered them in the right direction to get help. I never told them about my private life but by then my occasional dates had progressed into a proper relationship. Playing the field had lost its appeal and I just had one goal in mind.

One lunchtime I could tell Judy wanted to say something. Eventually I coaxed it out of her.

"My sister says it's obvious things are getting serious and perhaps it's time to tell Ryan the truth."

"And what do you think?" I asked.

"That she's right, but I need to handle it carefully. You know, like we did with the rugby… drop hints and let him make up his mind calmly without me trying to push him."

"So, we need a plan?"

We arranged that she'd drop Ryan at practise a bit earlier than usual. Before he got out the car, she'd say there was someone she'd like him to meet afterwards. That would give him two and a half hours to get a little accustomed to the idea that he wasn't the only male in his mother's life.

I saw Judy drive up. She'd only switched off the engine for a moment when Ryan leaped out, slammed the door and came running over to me.

He was so agitated I wouldn't have understood what he was trying to say if I'd not had a good idea what was troubling him. If the words I did catch were anything to go by, it was a mercy most of it was unintelligible.

As I'd planned, I let him vent until he had himself more or less under control. The idea was that when he spoke to his mum again he'd be in a more receptive frame of mind. Once he'd stopped yelling I asked if he still wanted to play. Admittedly it wasn't a fair question. If he didn't he wouldn't be in the team for the big game.

"Yeah, I'm playing but I won't get in the car when she comes to pick me up!"

"I'm giving you a lift home." This was part of the plan I'd arranged with Judy.

"You? Why you?"

"Think about it, Ryan."

"It's you? You're going out with my mum?"

His immediately jumping to that conclusion hadn't been part of my plan. I didn't reply. Nothing I could have said at that point would have helped as he was no longer listening.

Once again his words tumbled over themselves. Maybe they didn't make any sense to him either, but the emotion was clear enough.

Eventually he snarled, "You tricked me! I thought you were on my side…"

"This isn't about me!"

"NO?"

"No. It's about your selfish attitude to your mother. She's hurting too and she's lonely. You won't stay with her forever will you?"

He shrugged, not meeting my gaze.

"But you expect her to always be there, alone, waiting for when you get in from school or matches. Then maybe you'll join a team or it'll be some other kind of work and you'll move out, maybe get married and what about her then?"

I saw he hadn't thought any of this through, but was beginning to.

By then the rest of the lads were arriving. I turned to face them and reminded everyone of my rule. "No training today, no selection for Saturday. Are we clear?"

There was a general, slightly confused, "Yes coach," as though they were aware they'd missed something, but couldn't figure out what.

"Well don't just stand there, get warmed up."

As I'd hoped, when the others jogged off, Ryan followed. He called me something unpleasant as he passed by, but I pretended not to hear.

As usual after practice, I waited until everyone had been picked up or cycled off. I wouldn't want to leave one of them stranded. Ryan hung around until it was just the two of us. Without speaking to him, I got in my car and waited.

He followed me. "I suppose if I don't get in you'll leave me out of the team on Saturday?"

"I haven't said you'll be in it yet."

He tried to speak but I didn't let him.

"I have decided, and whether or not you accept a lift home won't make any difference. Not to me. Your mum will be put out though. She asked me to give you a lift so she could put the finishing touches to the dinner she's making. This evening is important to her, Ryan."

"And what about me?" He didn't sound angry anymore. He sounded like a scared little kid.

"Not everything is about you. Your mum wants a relationship for herself, not to hurt you. She wouldn't marry someone you hated or who'd mistreat you, but you won't let her get close to anyone at all, not even someone you'd like and who could help you."

"Like you?"

"I hope I have helped you."

"I suppose. You did trick me though. Why didn't you tell me you were dating my mum?"

"Because I'm not. "

"But. You … I… "

"You jumped to that conclusion and lashed out before you'd even thought about it long enough to realise it isn't true. Your mum's boyfriend is called Jake, she's been seeing him for a long time. I think you met him once?"

"Sort of. I told him to clear off and I thought he dumped her." It was clear he didn't remember the incident with pride.

"No, just backed off a bit, so as not to upset you. He sounds like a good chap. Would it hurt you to meet him and be civil long enough to decide if you agree?"

"I suppose not."

He didn't speak on the drive to his home. Neither did I until I pulled up outside. "Ryan, if you do happen to like Jake, see if he wants to come and watch you play on Saturday."

"I'm playing?"The joy shining in his eyes told me Judy's evening was going to be a success.

I hoped the same would be true of mine. I intended to ask Louisa, my flame haired nurse, two important questions; would she come to Saturday's game and would she do so as my fiancée?

13. Learning To Handle It

When I told Neil that I'd decided to 'face my fear', he looked delighted, then very quickly seemed to be trying to hide that reaction. He took my hands and looked closely into my face. "Are you absolutely sure? I'll buy you a drink and you can wait in the beer tent if you'd rather." As a six-foot-four copper there's not much which scares him, but that doesn't make him insensitive to the concerns of others.

"I've only got to walk a little way. I'll be fine," I told him with more confidence than I felt. "Not that I'm saying no to the drink. Can we have one together later?"

"It's a promise. I might even stretch to prosecco and a prawn sandwich."

We'd only been together a couple of months, but he already knew me pretty well! We were at the County Show, with some of Neil's workmates. It wasn't a date precisely, but he'd invited me along.

"We'll be working on a stand, talking to members of the public – just letting them see we're good guys," he'd explained. "We're all taking turns, so I'll have time to look round with you too. Being seen in uniform, doing what everyone else does, is part of it."

Another part was giving out stickers, letting kids try on his hat, set off the siren and pat police dogs. At first I'd said

I couldn't be involved in that, but didn't mind waiting. Then I decided to do more than just sit on a straw bale…

I adjust the shoulder strap on my bag, take a deep breath and say, "OK, I'm ready."

"My brave Angie." Neil pecks me on the cheek, lifts the rope of the enclosure for me to duck under, and rejoins his colleagues.

I don't feel particularly brave, but I'm not terrified. The reassuring police presence helps. Even if he isn't right by my side, I know Neil won't let any harm come to me. The same applies to his colleagues.

I take a few tentative steps, all on my own. The sun is shining on my back, the grass is springy under my feet and I feel pretty much OK. After a few steps I'm relaxed enough to take in my surroundings, noticing the brightly coloured Helter Skelter in the distance and the banner marking the beer tent. I feel myself smile at the thought of heading there later with Neil. Then it happens.

Someone snatches at my bag, jerks the strap off my shoulder and runs away with it.

"Stop!" someone yells. Not me, I'm too surprised to do anything. Not just surprised. I tense up and can't move. I tell myself to be as brave as Neil thinks I am.

He wasn't always brave himself. He told me he grew up being scared of the police!

"We lived in a rough area and, for many of the neighbours, the arrival of the police always meant trouble. Mum said they were the good guys but I had difficulty accepting it."

"What changed?" I'd asked.

"One day Mum took me to the County Show. I got lost and panicked. A police officer looked after me and got someone to call for Mum on the loudspeakers. I saw she was right, they were the good guys."

It was then I'd told him about my own issue. "I'm sort of the opposite of you. Mum had a bad experience once, which made her anxious on my behalf, so I learned to be nervous from her. People tell me I don't need to be scared and I sort of know it's true, but I want proof."

Neil had offered me today's opportunity to experience that, but made it clear the choice was mine. I'd agreed and now…

A huge dark mass of fur whooshes right past me. The massive Alsatian leaps at the thief, grabs him by the arm and brings him down. I join in the cheers of the crowd. My fear not entirely gone, but well under control, I walk slowly to where the thief is being handcuffed.

Playing the part of the victim in the police display has helped me see some dogs are the good guys. I'm pretty sure I'm going to be able to give my rescuer a quick pat of thanks, before Neil takes me to the beer tent. Over that prosecco and prawn sandwich, we'll celebrate me starting to overcome my fear, and Neil's transfer and start of his training as a police dog handler.

14. Dancing Into The Future

Ginny and Robert's wedding invite unsettled me. It made me feel I'm part of the past, and caused me to worry about them. Robert is my only grandson. Ginny's my goddaughter. I went to school with the grandmother she lost when just a baby and have done my best to make up for that lack.

I didn't encourage them to get together. Not because I had anything against the idea, it just never occurred to me it might work. They're so different in personality, upbringing and everyday life. Robert's the only child of a single mother, who has remarried and moved away. Ginny, baby sister to three siblings, was still living with her parents in their huge home when they started dating. She was surrounded by indulgent aunts and uncles too. Her wages were all pocket money to her. If she got bored with a job she packed it in. Everything Robert earned was needed for rent and food. He couldn't just quit, so he'd been a conscientious employee who was starting to rise in the company.

When they started going out, it seemed I was wrong in thinking their differences would be a problem.

"Her family make me feel so welcome and there are so many of them that there's always news, always something going on," Robert told me.

I could understand the appeal of that. When he comes to see me, which I'm pleased to say is quite often, I'm always just the same. Nothing interesting to report. Thankfully no bad news either. Although it gives me pleasure to hear he's healthy and happy and doing well at work, our conversations are never what you'd call exciting.

With Ginny it's different. Her visits to me are fleeting and infrequent, but filled with drama. She's always on her way to or from somewhere, sometimes both. In she'll burst with an armful of gifts. Flowers, chocolates, cakes, scented candles, glittering brooches, handmade soaps…

She collects pretty things wherever she goes, but her extravagance is matched by her generosity and she quickly dispenses her bounty amongst those she thinks will enjoy it.

The attractive nicknacks and tasty treats are accompanied by a torrent of information and opinion. "I just had to stop at this cute little gift shop, so important to support local businesses isn't it? Cousin Jackie needs all the customers she can get anyway, especially now she's pregnant again! Oh, but what a nightmare to park! Really something should be done."

I nodded in agreement, despite being unsure which shop has the parking problem and who should do what about it.

"I got you this," she passed me something wrapped in tissue paper. "I think it'll match the tiles in your bathroom." She was off to check, before I'd even seen what it was, and back to ask if she could fetch herself a glass of water a moment later.

"Goodness, child. Sit and catch your breath and I'll make us a cup of tea."

She obeyed, although she was already tapping away at her phone as I eased myself out of my seat and only put it away to take the tray from me as I came back into the room.

"Sorry, I meant to come and help."

"Don't worry. As I tell Robert often enough, I'm quite capable of boiling the kettle."

"Bet he still does it for you. He's so kind, isn't he?"

"He certainly is."

"And sensible too. I think his steadying influence might be good for me."

Again I agreed with her.

Robert had said her sense of fun was good for him. "I'm in danger of being dull."

I'd agreed with that too. He isn't dull, but with just work and me for company, he could end up that way. To me he's perfect. Always studied hard, always remembers birthdays and obligations. Always on time. But I can see others might think him almost boring. Ginny can be a bit scatty and a touch irresponsible, but she's a ray of sunshine. You can't help liking her and I'm not surprised her well-off family so often indulged her whims. If I had the means to write a cheque for something which would give her a moment's pleasure, I'd do it too.

When they got engaged I was delighted. The wedding invitation worried me a little though. Everything seemed so extravagant compared to how things had been in my day. So different. When I married, we'd had a simple church service, followed by a buffet in the village hall and dancing to Dad's record player. We danced so often together in that hall, sometimes to real bands, but that first time as man and wife is the one I remember best.

The wedding day itself was wonderful. Robert and Ginny got married in a restored castle and had a fancy sit down meal, then dancing to half an orchestra. Everyone was so happy, but something troubled me. I didn't begrudge them,

I'm sure it wasn't that, but it did seem a waste of money. Maybe because I'd never had much. And neither has Robert.

I was delighted to watch the newlyweds uphold tradition and perform a proper first dance – a waltz. It was wonderful to watch.

Dancing is one of my great joys and always has been. For my husband and me it was our one extravagance, and in my younger days I was really good, with trophies to prove it. I still dance now. On Tuesday and Thursday evenings and Sunday afternoons a group of us get together and dance to records. Some of us are better than others, but we all enjoy it. Now dancing is popular again on TV it helps us feel in touch with the modern world, and seeing that Robert and Ginny were interested, made me feel more in touch with them.

Robert apologised for not asking me to help them learn. "We wanted it to be a surprise. I hope you don't mind?"

"Of course not! It was a lovely surprise."

It was another lovely surprise when they came to visit me shortly after the honeymoon, bringing photographs. I imagined they'd be too busy with their new life, new home and old jobs to spare me much time, but they continued to visit as often as before.

It didn't take many months to realise my concerns over their marriage had been justified. Money was the biggest reason for friction. Between them they earned all they needed and a little left over. Robert wanted to save every penny of it, but never got the chance because Ginny spent the surplus, and more, before it reached their joint account.

I was showing Ginny that I'd put her wedding photos in the album along with those taken on my fortieth anniversary, when she asked if I had any tips for staying happily married for so long. That gave me the chance to explain a little about Robert's pride and how he wanted them to support themselves, not rely on handouts from her parents at the end of each month.

"Oh dear. I've just carried on doing what I've always done and not thought how it might feel to Robert. I'd better try to keep my spending under control, hadn't I?"

She did her best and mostly it was pretty good. As an example, she finally took notice of my saying I valued her presence more highly than her presents. Instead of coming to see me laden with gifts, she brought colour charts and catalogues to show me what she hoped to do with their house. I was pleased she was willing to wait for at least some of the changes. Being able to help pleased me even more.

"That's a huge price to pay for curtains," I said one evening. "Especially as you already have some." I'd seen them and very nice they were, even though they were mostly far too long for the windows.

"I know, but the cottage windows aren't a standard size, so we need tailor made."

"Nonsense, just alter those you have."

"Oh! Yes, perhaps I could."

Turns out she's good with a needle. That fancy school she'd gone to taught her how to embroider, so it just needed a few tips from me to show her how to put those skills to good use. I can't imagine Ginny ever darning socks, but now I know she won't throw away a designer suit because a button comes loose.

OK, so she did get the crafting bug and buy lots of ribbons and the like to make tiebacks and trim light shades and goodness knows what else, but the cost was low, for her, and gave a great deal of pleasure.

Getting Robert to lighten up was more of a struggle. I did hint he allow his wife to have some fun, without criticising every extravagance. Yes, going out to dinner several times a week wasn't possible on their joint income, but a coffee or glass of wine now and again surely was. I'm careful myself, but if there's any of my pension left at the end of the month, I've been known to pop into the tearooms in town and treat myself to a cream slice.

"I could buy a whole bottle of wine for the price of one small glass in the pub," Robert pointed out.

"It's not just about the wine," I explained. Ginny was used to parties and weekends away with her friends. She didn't do that once she was married, but it seemed a mistake to replace her entire social life with evenings in the supermarket looking for offers.

I thought of suggesting they join our Sunday dances, but was reluctant to interfere more than I already had. Perhaps it wasn't really that. They wouldn't have been rude, but I worried about their possible reaction. We tell ourselves that through the dancing we're enjoying the present moment, but are we? Perhaps we're just reliving the past. A past which has no place in the future of two people I care so much about.

I thought Robert was beginning to understand until Ginny turned up and said they'd rowed. Although naturally disturbed to hear they'd quarrelled, I was glad I was hearing it, if you follow my meaning. If I could help these two young people, I was still relevant, part of the present.

"So, you came to me?" I asked as I settled her on the sofa with a cup of tea.

"I thought this is where Robert would come." She gave a stifled sob. "I don't know him as well as I thought, do I?"

Nor me it seemed. I too had thought I'd be the one he turned to if upset – after Ginny herself of course.

"I was going to go to my mum or sisters, but really it's him I need to talk to, to sort things out, isn't it?"

It seemed I didn't know her as well as I'd thought either. She was more mature than I'd given her credit for. They'd rowed over money she told me. "You probably know about Robert's savings scheme he pays into each month?"

"I do, yes." He'd started it when he first started working. The £60 a month seemed quite a lot then and earned a little interest. It wasn't due to pay out for years. "Robert always intended it would pay a chunk off the mortgage," I said.

"I know and he doesn't want me to spend more than we earn. I get that now."

She wanted to cash in the savings scheme! I suppose in her world of having whatever she wanted the moment she wanted it, that seemed perfectly logical. What could she want the money for? Last week she was telling me about the Caribbean holiday her unmarried girlfriends had booked and the week before she referred to her two-year-old car as though it were ancient.

"I suggested we took dancing lessons," Ginny said. "You know, continue on from what we learned for the wedding. We both took to it pretty well, I thought?"

I agreed they had and learning to dance together did seem like a fun thing to do and that yes, it would be good exercise and was more sensible than going out drinking, or eating big meals at even bigger restaurant prices. However I could see the advantage of keeping the saving scheme running too.

"It's a bit like marriage," I said. "You've invested a lot of time and money starting up a relationship, having that fabulous wedding, setting up your home. You're not going to throw all that away over a temporary row, are you?"

"No, definitely not… and Robert is so sensible and practical, he won't want to either will he?"

"I'm sure he won't."

"And you'll help me persuade him not to spend his savings?"

Before I could ask what she meant, Robert came in. He headed straight to the kitchen and I joined him. As he filled the kettle and set out mugs, he explained he and Ginny had rowed. "I can't find her to apologise. I went to her mum and we called all her sisters, but no luck."

She appeared, "And I came here, looking for you."

I could see she was relieved that she did know him and from the way they hugged I felt sure they'd work out their problems.

"You two sit down, I'll see to the tea." I was careful to take a long time about it. I couldn't help overhearing a lot of their conversation though. It seemed Ginny had discovered Robert in the process of booking a cruise which included daily dance lessons because he thought that's what his wife wanted.

Ginny had been both horrified at the cost and hurt he hadn't realised she'd grown up at last. "You talked before about us being a team and managing without Dad's cheque book, then you tried to do this without even telling me."

"I wanted it to be a surprise."

"I expect the cost of new ballgowns would have been a surprise too! I'd have needed those for the cruise." Then in a gentler voice she added, "Sorry, Rob. I know you were trying to be nice, but you don't have to buy my love, and thanks to your gran I've realised we don't always have to spend money to be happy."

I didn't hear the next part. When I came back, the reconciliation seemed complete and they were making plans.

Ginny asked, "Do you think we could join your Sunday tea dances?"

"Of course. The events are public really, even though it's only the same old crowd who attend."

Robert asked if anyone there might be prepared to teach them some steps.

"There won't be a problem about that."

Actually as soon as I said it I realised there might be. Everyone would be keen to teach them and be a part of their progress, so there would be friendly rivalry over who got the honours.

"Would it be too cheeky of me to ask if I could borrow something to wear?" Ginny said. "I've got a couple of nice dresses, but if we're going to dance regularly it would be good to have more. I remember when I bought you those scented hangers for your gorgeous dresses you said you weren't sure why you kept the ones which no longer fit. I'm quite a bit slimmer than you and ...oh dear! That was cheeky too."

I assured her she wasn't being cheeky and I'd be happy to lend her something. "If you can hem curtains and make those fancy trimmings, I dare say you'll manage to take in a dress." I'll be happy to help too and for her to wear the beautiful clothes I've kept packed away in tissue paper and lavender. For them, and my grandson and his bride, to dance into the future and for me to be a tiny part of that.

15. Rowing To America

Almost every evening throughout the winter, Ethel heard a strange sawing noise. It wasn't loud, but she couldn't quite ignore it. None of the neighbours seemed to be carrying out big DIY projects; she'd have seen them unloading supplies. Perhaps somebody had begun making jigsaws as a hobby, but would they do that for precisely one hour each night?

Ethel got her answer when the days lengthened. The boy across the road was using a rowing machine in his lounge. What a waste of energy. Ethel was surprised as he seemed sensible in other ways. She'd spotted his washing hanging on the line which was much better than getting it creased in a tumble drier. He travelled by bus rather than bothering with a car which wouldn't be practical in the heart of the city.

On an unseasonally warm spring day, he was rowing with his window open. Ethel went over and called out. "What's the point of that? It won't get you very far!"

"Yes it will – America!" he'd replied.

"Cheeky boy!"

"I'm thirty-seven."

Ethel stomped off back home.

The following day she visited the library to look up how far it was to America. The boy meant he was doing the equivalent distance she supposed, though why he felt that was worthwhile she had no idea. Even to the nearest bit it was over 4,000 miles.

That evening she crossed the road again. "How far do you go each day?" she demanded.

He wiped his hands on a towel and stuck his sweaty arm out the window. "Good evening. I'm Mark."

Ethel shook hands briskly. "Miss Reynolds."

"Nice to meet you, Miss Reynolds. On average I manage about six kilometres."

Ethel wasn't sure how many miles there were in a kilometre, but even so the maths was easy. "It will take forever."

"I've been doing it a long time. Should get there about a year from now."

Did he have an answer for everything? It seemed he did, as whenever she asked how he was getting on he reported seeing dolphins, conning towers of submarines or flying fish. So silly!

"Have you gone round the Cape yet?" she asked one evening.

"Won't be long now!"

Ethel admitted she didn't really know what it meant. "Just something I heard on TV."

"Dangerous stretch of water."

"You be careful!" How odd; she was joining in his daft game. It would seem she actually liked him.

The next evening she suggested he exercised outside in the fresh air.

"I row with the window open."

"That's not the same. Anyway, shut in there you don't meet people."

"I've met you Mrs R."

"It's Miss Reynolds, but you may as well call me Ethel."

So, they were on first name terms. Friends almost. A bit like Lucy down the library who helped Ethel look up the various creatures and places Mark mentioned. Lucy also suggested books Ethel might like to borrow, so she'd joined the library, and the book group. Her trips across the road to question Mark had got her talking to her neighbours too. She'd even started baking now the cakes would be eaten before they went stale. It seemed that ridiculous rowing was doing her good, even if it wasn't doing anything for him.

"Why don't you use your energy doing something useful?" she asked Mark, over a slice of lemon drizzle.

"Like cutting your grass, Ethel?"

"Now you mention it…"

"Tell you what, I'll cut your grass when I'm here, and when I'm away you can water my hanging baskets. Deal?"

"Deal." He'd never gone away as far as she could recall and even if he made a regular thing of it she'd be quite happy to do the watering; even look after the house if he wanted.

Months later he came round with his keys and told her he'd left a small watering can by the water butt.

"Oh! Right, OK. Where are you going?"

"I keep telling you!"

"America?"

"Yes. My rowing machine is set up with a dynamo, so I power the house lights and a few other things. I've saved the money and booked a holiday."

16. Pastures New

"Walking to work is doing me good," Saffron said. "I feel much fitter."

Grant barely glanced at her before returning his attention to his breakfast. "You look better too," he mumbled into his cereal.

Saffron was too surprised to answer. She hadn't been fishing for compliments and in the two years Grant had been her lodger she'd got used to getting very little reaction from him. Actually he'd always been like that. He'd been her first boyfriend, when she was just fifteen, and even then he'd been reserved.

With some people Saffron would have taken the remark as criticism of her appearance before she'd begun to take regular exercise, but not with him. Grant was never unkind; she wouldn't have agreed to him having her spare room if he was, but the lack of emotion which seemed cool when they were teenagers, felt almost cold thirty years later. She wanted warmth.

Saffron washed her bowl and mug and left them on the drainer. "I'll get off then." It was earlier than usual, but she thought it better to go before she read too much into his remark and embarrassed them both – again. Besides, part of her route was across farmland. It would be nice to take her time and look out for signs of spring in the hedgerows.

On her way to work Saffron was temporarily delayed by a lorry backing across the footpath through the field. From the noise coming from the back she guessed it contained cows.

"Sorry to hold you up," the farmer said.

"I'm not really in a hurry," Saffron assured him.

"In that case you might want to stick around and watch when I let them out. They always make me laugh."

"Cows make you laugh?" Saffron asked.

"You'll see."

Naturally she had to wait to find out if they really would do anything amusing.

The farmer released the lorry's tailgate, which formed a ramp down to the ground. A big black and white head looked out. Soon there was another, then a third animal pushed between them and out onto the ramp. Its first steps were tentative but once it reached level ground the animal shot away doing a spirited imitation of a bucking bronco.

The mooing got considerably louder, but didn't drown the sound of the animals jostling for position in the lorry. Soon all the cattle had negotiated the ramp and were leaping around like excited puppies. The sight was indeed funny and Saffron chuckled at their antics. She was glad though that all the activity was taking place at a safe distance. The animals could easily knock her down and didn't seem to be taking much notice where they were going.

"I have to keep them inside over winter to protect them from cold, and feed them," the farmer said. "But I love letting them out in the spring."

"It seems they share the feeling." Saffron could feel their joy at being out in the spring sunshine and laughed as they jumped over nothing and kicked out at fresh air. She and the farmer watched until the animals settled down to eat grass.

On her way back home that afternoon the cattle were at the further end of the field. Most continued to eat, but now and then one raced round in a circle, clearly not yet over the novelty of relative freedom. A few looked her way as she passed through their territory but otherwise they ignored her. Perhaps to avoid comparisons with life at home, Saffron thought about what the farmer said that morning. He obviously looked after his animals well, but she knew not all were so lucky. Some were factory farmed; kept in all year round, with barely room to move. It wasn't a nice thought.

That evening Saffron told Grant about the cattle and how funny they looked.

He grinned. "I'd like to have seen that."

"They seem to have settled down now, but the farmer said they're inquisitive and might follow me for the first couple of days."

"Maybe I could walk part of the way with you tomorrow morning and see them for myself?"

"Oh. Yes, if you like."

When the cattle crowded around her the next morning she was more than usually grateful for his company. If she'd been on her own their behaviour might have felt more threatening than simple nosiness. With him there it seemed comical to have the creatures watching her almost as though mirroring her inspection of them the previous day.

When one got a little too close for comfort, she shooed it away and laughed as it backed up a couple of spaces before wandering off as though proving it wasn't really all that interested anyway.

Saffron guessed Grant's reason for accompanying her was protective. She hoped he was also motivated by the chance to spend more time with her. "Thanks for walking with me," she said.

"I thought getting some exercise would be good for me too. I've put on a few pounds lately."

That was true, but it suited him. "I hope you didn't think I was trying to suggest that?"

"I thought you might be concerned about the health of an old friend."

"No! I mean yes, but… " She always got tangled up when she tried to discuss their relationship. Time to change the subject. "Umm, Grant?"

"Yes?"

"I've been thinking, I'd rather only buy free range meat and milk from now on." She never had bought eggs from caged birds, as she'd found out at school exactly how appalling the conditions were. Now it seemed right to extend that to include all animals which provided her with food.

"Fine with me," Grant said.

"It will cost more."

"I'll put another fifty a month in. Will that cover it?"

Saffron guessed that would be more than enough for both of them and knew that if it wasn't he'd agree to however much she asked. He was generous; with money at least. True he had plenty of it, but that didn't always make people more willing to share.

Grant's generosity was another of his traits which hadn't changed over the years. At sixteen he'd stayed at school whilst Saffron started working in a shop. Although she had more money than him in those days, he'd often used what he earned from his part time job to buy her flowers or gifts and he'd paid his way whenever they went out.

They did that far less often and were drifting apart by the time he went to university. It was a long way for him to travel just to spend a few hours with her and they both agreed he should concentrate on his studies rather than make the journey every week.

Maybe she'd been a bit hasty breaking up with Grant before they'd even tried to make it work, but surely it was better to stay on good terms than to make unreasonable demands and end up rowing? That really might have harmed his education. As it was she'd kept in touch with Grant. He even came to her and Chris's wedding.

After university, Grant had worked on oil rigs as an engineer. It was very well paid. He worked long hours when actually out on a rig, but had breaks of several weeks between those stints. On his time off he travelled; cruises, safaris, hotels on glorious beaches. Over the years, Grant visited Saffron and Chris, bringing her a lavish gift and taking them both out for a meal in one of the best local restaurants.

Then Chris died. Grant was on a rig at sea, but sent a message of condolence and said if there was anything he could do, to let him know. Lots of people made the same offer but there wasn't anything anyone could do to ease her grief. Not at first.

Her parents and friends helped her get through all the formalities and then to pick up some of the pieces of her life. She returned to work, cooked herself meals and pretended to be OK. On good days she even convinced herself.

After the first shock of being a widow was over, Saffron's biggest problem was loneliness. Some mornings the realisation that the house would be empty when she returned made it difficult to walk out the door. She'd asked Grant to stay, the next time he was off work.

He'd hugged her tight when he arrived; the first, and last, time he'd held her since they were teenagers. He let her cry before again offering to help in any way he could. "You know I earn more than I can spend, so…"

"Thanks, Grant but I'm OK for money. I just miss Chris."

"Of course you do. There's nothing I can do about that, but I would if I could."

"You are helping. It's not so hard going off to work or the shops if I'm not dreading coming home to an empty house. Difficult for you to understand I suppose, as you travel alone so much, but I've never lived alone."

One day he said, "Think about it before you answer, but how would you feel about having me here permanently?" Grant asked.

"As a base when you're off the rigs you mean?" He'd be away a lot more than he was there, but it might help to know he would be coming back.

"Not exactly. I'm getting fed up with not having a home of my own and the job isn't as much fun as it was when I started out. I fancy a change."

"You're not just saying that for my benefit?" Saffron asked.

"No. I wasn't necessarily going to do it quite yet, but I had planned to leave the rigs before it was too late to do anything else and there's no reason to put it off."

"And you intended to come back to this area?"

"It's the closest I have to home and you're the nearest I have to family."

"Oh." Never before had it occurred to her that he too must be lonely.

"Plus I've never had to cook or shop or do housework. Don't know where to start, so you'd be doing me a huge favour if you let me stay here."

"OK, I'll think about it."

It hadn't taken her long to decide and for them to settle into a comfortable routine. She worked, cooked and cleaned. He took a few freelance consultation jobs, paid the bills and took her to dinner whenever she agreed to go. It was a bit like her interaction with the cattle in the field she walked through twice a day. At first they were slightly wary of each other and treading carefully, but they took less notice each day and she soon got used to them as part of her life. When one blocked access to the stile so she couldn't get out the field, she just pushed it gently and it obligingly moved.

Grant was just like that. He did his own thing, but if she asked anything of him he quickly complied. For a long while that had suited her perfectly. She had the emotional space to grieve for Chris, yet had the comfort of a friend who was physically close. She didn't forget her husband or stop loving him, but the feelings she'd had for Grant when they were teenagers returned. They seemed to have matured and strengthened over the years. So far her attempts to discover if he felt the same way, without risking losing him completely if not, hadn't gone well.

Saffron had met the farmer twice more over the summer and she had a much better idea how he felt about her than she did with Grant. On each occasion since their first meeting the farmer had chatted pleasantly and mentioned his wife, so she knew he didn't intend anything more than a very casual friendship. Did Grant? He'd had girlfriends in the past, but if he'd dated anyone since he'd moved in with her, he hadn't mentioned it. Was he being tactful, or was she the only woman in his life? And if so, what did that mean?

It was a Friday afternoon in late autumn when Saffron met the farmer for the fourth time. Once again he'd backed the lorry into the field. This time he had two people with him and they'd set up a kind of pen made from gates. The day was grey, the trees bare and field muddy. The cattle moved slowly as they were herded into the pen and then back into the lorry. Quite a contrast with the joyful sight of them being let out six months previously.

"Are they going into the barn for the winter?" Saffron asked the farmer.

He shook his head.

"Where then? Oh…" She trailed off as the answer dawned on her. They were to be killed for meat.

The farmer must have seen she'd worked it out and that she was upset. "I don't have any choice. These are all steers; no good for milking or breeding."

She'd vaguely realised that them being raised for beef was a possibility, but had pushed the thought away. Just as when she bought meat in the supermarket she pictured a meal, rather than the live animal.

Saffron wanted a hug and rushed home to Grant. She blurted out what she'd seen and heard, half wondering if he'd think she was being naively sentimental.

Grant gently pointed out the farmer was right. "The alternative to growing them on for beef would be to kill most male calves at birth. These have had a happyish life, haven't they? That's better?"

"I suppose… They really did seem content over the summer."

Even so, when she prepared their planned meal of ham, egg and chips she didn't put any ham on her own plate. On Saturday she made macaroni cheese.

"Lovely," Grant said as he scraped up the crispy pieces of cheese from the edge of the dish. "I haven't had that for years. Not since I came round to yours and your mum cooked it, I don't think."

"You remember what you ate all that time ago?"

"Your mum's meals stood out. The food in the care home was whatever would fill us up, could be eaten by everyone and produced within a tight budget, so generally wasn't very tasty."

His childhood probably explained Grant's fondness for eating out in restaurants, especially those serving unusual food. It explained other things too, like the way that whenever she was upset he'd talk it through with her and try to find a practical solution, rather than give her a big hug and make unrealistic promises that everything would be OK. And how he kept his feelings to himself and didn't risk hurting or being hurt emotionally.

Saffron did want him to hug her. Not just when she was upset and not just as a friend. She needed to find a way to let him know that without running the risk of losing him altogether if he didn't feel the same way.

"That smells good," Grant said on Sunday lunchtime. "Meat loaf?"

"Nut roast."

"Oh, right."

"I've never made it before, so I don't know what it will be like."

"You know me, always happy to try something new."

"Yes, you're adventurous… when it comes to food."

"That's because I have the luxury of knowing that if I don't like it, I can just buy something else."

Good point. And if he, or she, were to mess up their current friendship by making unwelcome advances he could buy himself somewhere else to live. But he wouldn't have a home. Saffron didn't want that to happen. If only she knew how he felt!

She was agitated all afternoon and didn't sleep well that night. On Monday morning the familiar dread she'd felt after losing Chris was back. Nothing like as strong, but that kind of feeling. She didn't want to leave the house, for fear it would be empty when she returned. What was wrong with her? Had she had a bad dream which still lingered in her memory? Maybe she was becoming agoraphobic.

Somehow she forced herself to smile at breakfast and tell herself it was just the awful weather making her reluctant to go out.

"It's tipping down. Let me give you a lift for once," Grant said.

"Thank you."

It helped and by the time she got to her desk, she'd almost convinced herself she was over the morning's silliness.

When she finished for the day, she found Grant waiting outside her office.

"Is something wrong?" Saffron asked.

"I didn't think you'd want to walk through the empty field on your own."

Of course! Grant had realised what was wrong, even though she hadn't. "How did you know?" she asked.

"Partly because of the switch to vegetarian food and you being upset this morning and... Let's just leave it there, shall we?"

"Why. If there's more, why not tell me, Grant? I always feel you're holding something back."

"There's a good reason for that." He shrugged then raised his hands in surrender. "If I were to behave as I want; to hold you tight to comfort you when you're upset, to dance around sharing your joy, you'd see that I care and that could make things awkward."

"So you do care and do want to do those things?"

He didn't meet her gaze, just gave the briefest of nods.

Grant turned to walk in the direction of the house, then stopped and reached for her hand. As they trudged back home, the sight of the muddy field saddened Saffron, but she recalled the animals leaping around in the spring sunshine and looked forward to seeing more do the same the following year.

"Umm, Grant?"

"What is it? If you'd like us to go permanently vegetarian, I think I can do that."

"I haven't decided about that, but there are parts of your suggestion I do like the sound of."

"Which parts?"

"Us and permanently," Saffron said.

"Does that mean ...?"

"That I love you? Yes."

"I love you too." He picked her up and swung her around, just as he'd done when, as a teenager, she'd first agreed to be his girlfriend. Once she remembered that, she realised he did show his emotions when it really mattered.

17. Call For Luvver Boy

Emma sighed. Yet another text from Alan! For weeks he'd bombarded her with calls; apologies, pleas to change her mind, or claims he'd found things belonging to her.

At first she'd replied as kindly as she could. "Don't worry, it's all in the past," and "It's over. Maybe it would help you to move on if we sold the house? It would certainly help me," and "I've already taken everything I want," were repeated frequently.

Martin, the new man in her life, pointed out Alan only started the calls after they'd got together. "He's just trying to cause trouble between us."

Emma wasn't sure about that, but it did seem Alan deeply regretted their split. That's probably why he was so reluctant to put the house on the market.

She'd considered changing her number, but so many people she wanted, or needed, to hear from would have to be informed. Besides she resented the idea of Alan still dictating her actions. When he called again she said, very firmly, she didn't want to hear from him and wouldn't answer further calls, nor reply to his texts.

It seemed he'd got the message, because for three days she didn't hear a word. Then she received a bouquet with the message, "Sorry I've been hassling you. I'll leave you alone now. I still love you and I've learned from my mistakes. Alan. X"

Had he? They'd been so happy once.

A week passed without him contacting her. His silence was almost disconcerting. That's why she read the latest text.

"Sorry I was difficult over the house. I'm ready to sell now. Can we talk?"

At last!

When she called, Alan said, "I don't want to end things in a solicitor's office. Can we sort out the paperwork over dinner?"

Not wishing to be as difficult as he once was, Emma reluctantly agreed.

At the restaurant, Alan answered a call while the waitress tried to take their order. He 'accidentally' took one brand new phone from his pocket, then swapped it for the even more expensive looking one which was actually ringing. As he explained he couldn't talk due to dealing with the sale of one of his houses, he fiddled with keys for a luxury car.

Emma was no more impressed by this show of wealth than the discovery there wasn't much to sort out. "This could have been dealt with over the phone in the time it took you to persuade me to come here."

"Maybe, but I wanted to see you again, Emma. I really do love you, unlike that new bloke of yours."

"Really?"

"Come on, if it's so great with him, why have you lied to him and come out with your ex?"

"I haven't. Martin knows where I am." And he hadn't made a massive fuss about it either, as Alan had whenever she'd even hinted at going anywhere without him. Martin's only concern was that she didn't let Alan upset her.

"Can't care much if he let you go out with another man," Alan said.

"He trusts me."

"Or has a reason for wanting you out the way?"

Emma rose to leave.

"I'm sorry. Don't go," Alan pleaded.

She wondered if he was just annoyed she wouldn't see him pay with a gold credit card, but a glance at his distraught face showed he realised he'd messed up. Again. Even so, she didn't stay for dessert.

Martin wasn't there when she got home. Two hours later he returned. "Just popped out for a quick beer."

The next day Martin laughed at a text he'd received and showed it to Emma. 'Thanks for a great night luvver boy. Must do it again soon. Sandra X X X'

"Someone made a big impression," he said.

"But not quite enough to make her remember his number?"

"Or lover boy isn't keen and gave her one of my business cards?" Martin suggested.

Emma felt some sympathy for Sandra, whoever she was. She sometimes wondered if Martin cared for her as much as she loved him. Admittedly it was a relief not to be smothered as she was with Alan. Probably Martin only seemed so casual in contrast.

Thankfully Alan hadn't changed his mind and a 'for sale' sign went up outside the house the next day. Soon after it was erected another bouquet and apologetic note arrived from Alan. Martin didn't give her flowers half as often as her ex did, but he didn't have anything to say sorry for, did he?

Poor Alan, he knew where he was going wrong, but didn't seem able to stop repeating his mistakes. If he carried on he'd never keep a girlfriend. That would be a shame as he had good points despite his distrusting nature. He was clever, and charming when he wanted to be. He used to be so much fun, often surprising her with trips away or thoughtful gifts and he'd brightened up boring days at work with jokes and flirty texts.

Emma spent several evenings on her own over the next week. Martin always seemed to be working late or out with mates. With the house still not sold they needed the overtime money and when they first got together she'd insisted they sometimes socialise separately to give each other space, but... Emma was lonely.

One evening Martin came home reeking of perfume. "Someone must have spilled it on me," he claimed.

That seemed an odd sort of accident, even to happen just once. One off, or even repeated, wrong numbers where much more likely. Even so, Martin was getting a lot. His phone beeped whilst he was showering before work. Emma, telling herself it could be urgent, picked it up and read, 'Hurry up luvver boy. I'm waiting here wearing just Channel No 5 and a big smile. Sandra X X X'

Emma made a note of the number, then put the phone back.

When Martin read the text he just grinned and said, "I'd better get off. Don't wait up." His jacket still smelled of perfume she noticed, as he pecked her cheek goodbye.

It was Emma's fourth evening in a row on her own. There was no housework left to do and nothing of interest on TV.

When Alan rang to say he had the sales details from the estate agent she was bored enough to agree to meet for a drink and have a look.

Alan was sweet. "I'll miss the house. We had some good times there, didn't we?" He spoke wistfully and, although he didn't say, she knew he missed her too.

"We did," she agreed.

"I hope you'll be just as happy in your new life, Emma," he said.

"Thank you. You too."

He shook his head sadly. "I've ruined my chance at that, but I hope we can stay friends. Remember I'll always care for you. I'll always be there if… well, if you ever need support."

"Why would I?"

He looked uncomfortable. "I don't know. Forget I said anything. I'm sure there's nothing in it anyway."

"Nothing in what?"

"Oh, well… there are rumours that new man of yours is cheating on you."

"If there's nothing in it why even mention it?"

"I shouldn't have. Sorry. Please forget I did."

Of course Emma couldn't forget. She hated feeling suspicious, but she was sure something wasn't right.

Martin was working late again when Alan rang asking her to come to Luigi's. "Just as friends."

It seemed harsh to remind him that the friends idea was his and she'd not agreed. Emma stumbled over a polite refusal.

"If you're busy I understand," Alan said.

"I'm not, but…"

"Come on, then. I know you like it there."

"I've never been."

"I thought I'd seen you there with your new man, um I mean… Sorry, my mistake, forget I said anything."

"Explain, Alan," Emma demanded.

"It's just that I saw your man with a woman and thought it was you. Obviously not. Maybe it wasn't him… or she could have been his sister?"

"He doesn't have one."

"Oh, right. Well obviously it wasn't him then. I mean, it can't have been, right?" He sounded quite upset. "I'm really sorry, Emma."

Less than ten minutes later, he was ringing the doorbell and offering flowers to apologise for hurting her. "I thought I was acting for the best in warning you about Sandra."

"Sandra?"

"That's the name of the girl people say he's been dating."

That confirmed it. Her suspicions were right! "Excuse me a minute, I'll just put these lovely flowers in water."

In the kitchen she typed into her phone, pressed dial and then returned to the lounge.

Alan's second phone must have been on silent, because Emma could only just make out a faint buzzing.

"That's 'Sandra's' phone, but the message is for you, Alan. It says never contact me again unless it's through your solicitor." She pointed to the door. "Now clear off and leave me to put on a big smile and Channel No 5 for my lover boy."

18. Fit Frida

As quite often happened, when Frida arrived at work, her boss Tobias was just ahead of her in the lobby. She wasn't entirely sure that was always coincidence. He pressed the lift call button, then turned to smile at her.

"Good morning, Frida. How was the wedding?" He blushed a little, but met her gaze.

"Lovely, thanks. Beautiful ceremony and my niece looked absolutely radiant." As they waited for the lift Frida told him how pretty her daughter Courtney looked as bridesmaid and how nice the food was at the reception.

"The profiteroles especially. Absolutely oozing with cream they were and dripping with chocolate." She'd eaten not only her own portion, but that of someone who'd declared she couldn't manage them as well as the canapés, prawn cocktail and Beef Wellington which had gone before.

"Mum," her son Charlie had murmured with a shake of his head as Frida said it would be a shame to waste them and stretched out her hand for the dish.

"Don't worry, love. They're already paid for, I'm not costing your cousin any extra."

Best not to think of the food; breakfast seemed a long time ago. Better to get Tobias interested in the reception, so she had a good excuse to show him the photos later on. They would include some of her looking her best. It had been a real struggle to find the perfect dress – she wasn't a size 12 anymore and the shops seemed to think everyone wanted skin tight clothing which showed more than it covered. Eventually she'd found a flattering, floaty peach outfit which was much smarter than her usual, bought for comfort, work clothes.

"The reception was in a marquee, decorated to look like a big top. My niece met her husband at a circus skills class apparently. Some people, including the bride and groom were juggling, walking on stilts and doing tricks on those bikes with just one wheel."

"A unicycle?"

"That's it. Looked quite comical, but hard work!"

"Was there dancing?" Tobias asked, his blush deepening and his gaze failing to meet hers.

Frida was used to this. His shyness wasn't crippling; when the conversation was work related he spoke confidently to everyone. He chatted socially with men, or ladies old enough to be his mother or young enough to be his daughter, without difficulty. It was only with women close to his own age he blushed furiously and couldn't look them in the eye.

That shyness was evident when he talked to Frida, but didn't stop him engaging in conversation, often initiating their chats. It was her secret hope he really liked her and so made that extra effort in her case. Really he'd like to ask her out, she told herself, but being her boss felt he couldn't. It was true the company frowned on such situations and would transfer one of the couple to a different department. For all Frida knew the rest of her fantasy could be accurate too. Maybe he imagined holding her close and swaying to romantic music, just as she dreamed of doing with him?

"There was. A real band!" Frida said as they stepped into the lift. "Ever so good they were, singing every song requested." She didn't mention she'd not actually danced to any of the tunes.

"I'm glad you enjoyed yourself," Tobias said as they reached their floor. "Have a good day." He strode quickly to his office, murmuring good mornings as he went. No one else was asked about their weekend.

Frida worked right through until twelve-thirty, only stopping a couple of times for coffee and biscuits.

"It's a lovely day," a colleague said. "Think I'll get some fresh air before I eat. How about you, Frida? Fancy a short walk?"

"No thanks. My sister promised to email me some wedding pictures and I want to look at those."

Frida munched a pork pie as she checked her emails. The pictures of the bride arriving, and Courtney carrying her train, were lovely. The first one showing Frida, a group shot outside the church, was rather unfortunate. She must have been much closer to the camera than everyone else as she looked huge! A shot of Frida with her two children in front of her was rather nice. She'd ask for a copy of that and get it framed.

Another email from Frida's sister contained more pictures, taken at the reception. As she flicked through Frida saw glimpses of herself. No, glimpse wasn't the right word, as there was a lot to see. The only positive was that she'd not bought the red and white dress she'd considered, thinking stripes might be flattering, as she'd have looked like a big top herself. Even so, there was no getting away from the fact she'd become fat Frida!

How could that have happened? She was quite trim until... She couldn't remember when things changed, but obviously they had. She'd always had a good appetite, but used to be very active too. Fit Frida everyone used to call her as she never waited for a bus if she could walk or cycle, joined in all the kid's games, went swimming, danced the night away at any social event. Why had no one told her how different she now looked? Not just come out with 'you're fat' of course. No one who cared enough to speak would be so cruel, but shouldn't they have dropped a few hints?

But they had, she now realised. At least tried to. The colleague who'd asked her to come for a walk had regularly made that suggestion. Her son Charlie often invited her to cycle alongside him as he jogged. Whenever Frida took Charlie and Courtney to Sunday lunch at her parents' home, the broccoli dish was placed nearest Frida and the roast potatoes furthest away. In the supermarket Courtney took charge of the trolley, loitering amongst the fresh veg and dashing through the bakery section.

Even Tobias had, in a way, given her a hint. She guessed he didn't make an effort to overcome his shyness because he was romantically interested in her. On the contrary he found her the easiest female member of staff to talk to as she was the least attractive!

That evening she told her children she was going to take their advice, lose weight and get fit. She had half the usual amount of potatoes with her tea, no bread and very little cola. The added lettuce and tomato filled the plate, but not her belly. It was really hard not to have something else as she washed up afterwards.

Later Charlie appeared, dressed for a jog. "Cycle along and be my personal trainer, Mum?" he suggested.

111

Why not? It would take her mind off how hungry she was.

The bike though wasn't in a fit state for use. "You go on, love. I'll pump up the tyres and oil the chain."

Frida did. She was out of breath by then, but determined to cycle, even if it was just to the end of the street and back. That proved more challenging than she'd anticipated. She had no trouble keeping the bike upright, at least for the first few hundred yards. After that she couldn't maintain sufficient speed and had to put her feet down and scoot herself back home. When she got off the bike her legs had turned to jelly and her breathing was a series of desperate gasps.

She was beginning to recover, but still sitting on the garage floor when Charlie got back. "You did it, Mum! Well done."

Frida confessed she'd only gone a very short way. She was about to say it was hopeless, she was starving hungry after cutting back for just one meal, and couldn't exercise for even five minutes, but Charlie reached out his hand and helped her up.

"The important thing is you've made a start. Keep going and it will get easier."

Her next work lunch included an apple in place of the crisps and was eaten after a short walk with her colleague. On the next shopping trip she half filled the trolley with vegetables and did the same to her plate each evening. She cycled a little further every day, and weaned herself off the cola. Charlie was right, it did get easier. Not easy – she could still only cycle for a few minutes and several times she'd realise she'd taken food from the cupboard and eaten it without noticing until she was holding an empty wrapper, but overall she was eating less and exercising more. Within days she felt less bloated and lethargic and was sleeping better than she had for years.

Frida, after braving the scales and checking the NHS website, calculated her target loss was just over three stone. After a month she'd lost two … pounds.

"Maybe the fat has turned to muscle?" she suggested doubtfully to Courtney.

"Don't forget you were gaining weight before," her daughter pointed out. "Taking that into account, you're really quite a bit lighter than you would have been."

That cheered Frida a little, and encouraged her to keep trying. The next week she lost two pounds and another the week after. It would have been more had she not got a voucher for half priced pizza. Progress felt slow, but there really was some and she definitely looked much healthier. Her skin, once greasy was now glowing. Previously tired eyes sparkled with energy and confidence. Frida noticed some of these improvements herself, but others told her too.

Tobias didn't say anything, at least not about her appearance. He still talked to her just as he'd always done; awkward enquiries about her weekend and children and more confident words about work. He suggested she apply for a promotion. That could have been taken as a hint he wanted her working elsewhere, but Frida was sure he was just being a good boss, trying to help a member of staff reach their full potential. Most likely that's all he'd ever been; a good boss who saw her as nothing more than a good employee.

Applying for promotion seemed a sensible idea. She was improving some aspects of her life, why not extend that to work? Tobias was her only reason for staying where she was and she'd been fooling herself about his feelings for her as surely as she'd been fooling herself over the pork pies and sweet drinks.

Tobias soon found a suitable post for which she could apply and helped her prepare for the interview. When appropriate he also invited her to work with him, showing her how and why he accomplished tasks, which meant she had a little experience of her hoped for new role.

The morning of the interview, Frida stepped on the scales. She'd lost an entire stone! It had taken months and would take many more before she reached her target weight, but she'd get there – and she'd get this job. Her confidence and enthusiasm seemed to impress the panel.

"Thank you," the chairman said afterwards. "We'll let you know our decision as soon as possible."

That afternoon Tobias approached her desk, holding a pristine white envelope. Her new contract, or a polite rejection?

"Congratulations, Frida. You made a really good impression and they'd like you to start as soon as that can be arranged."

Her colleagues congratulated her, but also assured her she would be missed. Tobias said nothing more, so she asked to speak to him privately.

"Of course," he said, leading her to his office.

"Thank you so much for all your help. I wouldn't have got this job without your support."

"Yes you would. You have all the skills required and the motivation to apply them."

"Even so, I'm grateful. Can I buy you a drink after work to say thank you?" What she didn't say, only half admitted to herself, was that it would be more than that to her. It would be a memory to hold onto, a mini fantasy of what might have been.

Tobias, blushing and looking intently at his desk, nodded an agreement.

"Great, see you in the lobby at five-thirty."

Frida returned to her desk, despite doubting she'd get any more work done. She was too full of emotion and her colleagues too full of congratulations and questions. As she talked and thought, she couldn't help glancing at the envelope Tobias had left. Instead of her full name typed out, it was hand addressed simply to Frida. The big dot over the i and looping a were just how Tobias wrote them when signing memos.

Ignoring everyone else, Frida ripped open the envelope and read the note.

Dearest Frida,

Until now our working relationship has meant I've kept my feelings for you a secret. Now things are about to change in that area, I feel free to speak. However my shyness means I'm doing so in writing. I hope you'll forgive that and agree to come to dinner with me?

Yours (I hope) Tobias.

19. More Than Numbers

Shaun had once hated his old maths teacher. In fact he'd wished Mr Flynn in his grave and had promised to celebrate when that happened. Now the old man was dead and the younger one sorrowfully heading towards the funeral and back into the past.

He'd been about thirteen when he was put into Mr Flynn's class. His parents and previous teachers had considered Shaun to be a genius at maths and he'd confidently expected the new teacher to be equally impressed. Mr Flynn had grudgingly conceded Shaun had an eye for numbers, but declared him to be lazy and unimaginative. The fact it was true made the words all the harder to hear. The knowledge he'd no longer get away with that was worse still. Gone were the days when Shaun's homework consisted of sums he could do in his head while unwrapping and eating a chocolate bar on the bus home.

Mr Flynn set him tasks which required thought. Instead of provably right answers he had to provide opinions and observations. Were mathematical sequences evident in nature? Did the golden ratio impact on his life? Even his favourite computer games were spoiled by the instruction to calculate his odds of success in various scenarios.

Even so, Mr Flynn frequently put him in detention for insufficient effort.

"It's not fair. No one else does the same amount of work as me," Shaun moaned.

"No, most of them work considerably harder," Mr Flynn declared.

Shaun had seen friends struggle to work out what was obvious to him in a glance and knew that was true.

"You think you're special, don't you, Shaun?"

"I'm a lot cleverer than most people."

"By most people, do you mean thirteen year old boys of your acquaintance?"

Admittedly that was the group he'd had in mind.

"And by a lot cleverer you mean you get the same answers to the same questions?"

He almost said he did it faster, but remembered the boys who beat him at running were no match for the likes of Coe, Cram and Ovett. Perhaps it was the realisation that the teacher understood him so well which made Shaun hate him.

"I wish you'd die so I could dance on your grave," he'd said.

Mr Flynn just smiled. "In that case, I have a little extra problem which I'm sure you'll enjoy." He wrote down his date of birth. "Using that and the assumption I reach the traditional three score years and ten, I'd like you to calculate how many hours you'll have to wait until you can tango across the churchyard."

To make matters worse, Mr Flynn didn't continue with his marking and leave Shaun to do his homework during detention as other teachers might. He insisted on lecturing Shaun about maths. According to Mr Flynn, the subject was responsible for pretty much everything. Even love.

"My wife is an architect," he explained. "Our shared appreciation of the golden ratio brought us together."

At the time Shaun had been as unimpressed by that as anything else the teacher told him. He'd been delighted when Mr Flynn retired the following year. At first the new teacher seemed so much better. Shaun was constantly praised despite putting in almost no effort. Trouble was the lesson and homework problems were so easy they actually seemed more boring than those set by Mr Flynn. Soon Shaun wasn't trying at all.

In detention again he'd explained and talked himself out of trouble and into a great deal more work. He'd grown up a little by then and realised good grades might equal a decent job.

At university Shaun discovered giving a girl chocolates or flowers won him a date. Presenting her with a book of poetry and telling her the golden ratio of the cover dimensions reminded him of the beauty of her smile, or walking along the beach with her explaining the mathematics behind spiral shaped shells, made a greater impression.

Thanks to maths, Shaun gained a job he loved designing computer games. And Julia. They'd married on another beach where she'd recited poetry as they exchanged rings. Maths had given him these things, but it was Mr Flynn who'd first let the subject reach him.

Shaun attended his teacher's funeral. Not to rejoice or dance on his grave, but to offer a quiet word of thanks – just as he had many times over the intervening years when the two men had formed a close friendship. Shaun placed a symmetrical shell on the coffin. Mr Flynn would have understood it represented more than numbers.

20. I Want Those Shoes!

When I first saw the shoes they were lying on the floor of the music shop's display window. They looked as though the mannequin had kicked them off just before I'd reached the bus stop. Obviously that hadn't happened. Mannequins can't flick their feet, even with someone manipulating their legs for them, and this one was being dressed, not undressed.

For the previous few weeks a male mannequin, dressed as Freddie Mercury, had posed in the window. I couldn't yet tell who this one was going to be. So far she wore nothing but a lemon coloured string bikini. By her side was a jumble of items, but I couldn't see what they were, except for the shoes. Perilously high stilettos in the tenderest of powder blue, with what looked like mother of pearl on the instep. They were absolutely beautiful and I wanted them.

"Suzie? Are you even listening to me?" my friend Alison interrupted my thoughts.

"Of course!" I exaggerated. Well, I had realised she was speaking, which sort of counts. "You were telling me about Pete taking you to Luigi's."

"No, I said I saw him in Luigi's with the redhead from accounts."

What! "Oh no! I'm really sorry."

She laughed. "Gotcha! I was just saying what we ate. Come on, what's got you all dewy eyed, and so distracted

119

that you don't notice whether or not your best friend's heart has been broken?"

"Shoes."

"Shoes?"

"Those shoes," I said pointing at them.

"Oh, nice."

"Nice? They're gorgeous. And I think they might be my size."

She glanced down at my comfy, padded ankle boots. "Maybe."

I understood her reaction. I'm not the sort who often goes into rhapsodies over anything so impractical. I don't recall ever feeling like that about a pair of shoes before. There have been some I'd wanted to put to use; wellies when the river burst its banks, anti-gravity shoes, some really funny musical slippers... But it was always for what they could do, not just because they were pretty. Alison and other friends have worn all kinds of pretty footwear which I've appreciated as items to give them pleasure, but not actually wanted for myself.

I recalled the last footwear which had attracted my attention. It was a pair of tatty hiking boots in this very window. There were two male mannequins on that occasion. They were dressed in very ordinary looking casual clothes and carrying placards with emphatic statements. I couldn't work out who they were supposed to be, but then I started wondering how many miles those boots had done.

"Hundreds, I should think," Alison said when I asked.

"Five hundred and then five hundred more!" I said, suddenly getting it.

"Oh yes, The Proclaimers. Very clever," Alison said.

Remembering that, I asked her if she could tell who the girl in the window was supposed to be. By then the mannequin had a pair of tartan trousers draped over one arm, and was holding up a shiny red dress with the other. We watched the window dresser as he put a pair of Elton John style sunglasses on her.

"What's the label say?" I asked Alison.

"25p. I don't get it. Come on, the bus is here."

The bus was pretty crowded, but I got my usual window seat in the front. From there I watched the young man slip the shoes onto the mannequin's uncooperative feet.

I was still thinking about the shoes at work, when a colleague said, "Penny for them?" She says that a lot and thinks that, as her name is Penny, this is hilarious. Actually it was quite funny the first time – and it's nice that she's interested in other people and laughs at herself. We don't all get it that way round, do we? I do try, but don't always succeed.

"Sorry, I was thinking about the most lovely pair of shoes I saw this morning."

"Shoes?" She was more than a little surprised.

"Yes, shoes," I said.

"Right. Sorry, Suzie… It's just that, no offence, you don't seem like you think much about clothes and things." She tried not to look at my baggy tracksuit as she said that.

I wasn't offended. Partly because I knew she hadn't meant to hurt me. Mostly because I understood her thinking it was true. Actually she was wrong. I think very carefully before buying any clothing. Like anyone else the colour is often what I notice first, but the look of the items is of far less importance to me than how easy they are to pull on and off, and that they be easily washed, with no need for ironing.

Please don't think I'm lazy – I just don't see the sense in making life more difficult than it needs to be. I suppose that's why I try not to take offence at innocently made comments, and not to be annoyed by oft repeated jokes. And, usually, not to want anything so impractical as palest blue, high heeled shoes.

"Ah, but you didn't see these shoes, Penny," I said. I described them in detail, including the fact that the surface looked like it might be soft to the touch. I had a moment of enlightenment – they were blue suede shoes! I felt sure all the other clothing the mannequin wore or carried would have featured in song lyrics. I kept that to myself though. Some of my colleagues find conversation with me awkward, even when I don't go off at a tangent, and I didn't want to make Penny feel awkward.

"They do sound nice," Penny said. "If it were me, I'd have to go back at lunchtime and buy them. I've seen fabulous shoes before and hesitated too long and missed out. I still regret missing a pair of turquoise strappy sandals, even though I'd wanted them to go with a dress that I had to throw out a couple of years ago."

"Should I do that? Go and see if I can buy them?"

She looked doubtful, just for a moment. "Yes. You're not like me, but if you want them and can afford them, I don't see why you shouldn't have them."

I could think of one reason – I hadn't spotted them in a shoe shop. That wasn't something I shared with Penny. It seemed a shame to spoil her realisation that, although obviously different in some ways, we had plenty in common.

"Thanks, Penny. I might just do that."

Back on the bus home, I asked Alison if she thought it was worth trying to buy shoes from a music shop.

"Yeah, I should think so. I've seen stuff from their window displays in the charity shop, so they'd probably sell it if anyone asked."

"I'll go in tonight then, just in case anyone else has the same idea."

"Want me to come with you?" she offered.

"Thanks, but I'll be fine and you need to get yourself beautiful for Pete."

"That doesn't take me long, I'll have you know!"

It takes no time at all because he knows her well enough to see she's beautiful on the inside. I don't say it though, she gets embarrassed by stuff like that. She'd do anything for me, except let me thank her.

Once I'd manoeuvred my way off the crowded bus Alison pretended to flounce away in a huff, which made me laugh.

I was grinning as I approached the music shop, and kept that up when someone kindly held the door open for me.

"How can I help, love?" He was the same man as I'd seen put those wonderful shoes onto hard plastic feet that morning.

"I've come about the shoes on the mannequin in the window. Blue suede, right?"

"Yep. Did you get the rest?"

"Red dress and teeny weeny yellow polka dot bikini and I guess the tartan trousers are Donald's?"

He nodded.

"It really is the shoes I'm interested in. Would I be able to buy them once the display comes down?"

"We usually get stuff from charity shops and send it back to another one. You can have them for a donation."

"Could I try them on and, if they fit, pay for them now? I don't want to miss out."

He shrugged. "Yeah, OK."

By the time he'd fetched them, I'd managed to get my warm and practical, yet ugly, padded boots off.

The assistant knelt at my feet and held one out, just as though it was a shoe shop. They were even lovelier close up. "Look about right, maybe just one size too large. Do you want me to …"

"Please," I said.

He was right, they were slightly on the big side, but that was good as it made them easier for him to slip onto my uncooperative feet. Other than that it didn't matter. It wasn't as though I'd ever walk anywhere in them and the footrests on my wheelchair would ensure they didn't slide off.

"I wish I could keep them now," I said.

"I'd let you if I had something else for the dummy's feet."

"Shame you don't still have those tatty boots The Proclaimers wore."

"Actually we do. Not even a charity shop wanted them but… Oh! Those boots were made for walking!"

By the time I'd wheeled myself out wearing the gorgeous stilettos, those old boots were lying on the floor of the music shop's display window, ready to be fitted onto the mannequin. The one wearing the outrageous glasses with the 25p price tag. Why such a low amount, I wondered.

When I finally remembered the ZZ Top song, Cheap Sunglasses I laughed and sang a few lines. People turned to look at me – probably admiring my lovely new shoes.

21. Lady In A Van

Little Mallow is my latest target. Although still charming, the village has more houses, a smaller pond and far bigger trees than when I was here last. There's a 'For Sale' sign which would have confused me for a moment, had I not known exactly what I'm here to do.

People usually aren't happy when I appear. They know absolutely nothing about me, where I've come from, what I've done or why I'm there, but the moment they see my campervan they decide they don't like me. This unreasonable suspicion makes things difficult for me at times, but I usually talk people round.

If there's a village shop, or post office which sells everything, I make that my first target. Little Mallow still has one, so in I go.

The shopkeeper greets me with, "Is there something I can help you with?"

"Just looking, thanks." Really I'm waiting for a bigger audience. It's not long in coming.

I ask for a piece of cheese and begin my spiel. "I love small shops like this where I can get a little of whatever I need. Supermarkets are cheaper if you buy multipacks, but that's not much help in a tiny campervan like mine."

That gets their attention. I can feel the silent, 'Ah, so we were right. She is responsible for the scruffy old van parked on the green'.

"There's not much storage," I continue. "Plus there's a limit to how much of the same thing one woman wants to eat."

Once they realise it's just me, not an extended family with multiple vans, they relax a little. Mentally upgrade my van from small and old, to vintage and cute. And so it is. Much more convenient than what I had before too.

I reach the most reassuring part of my well-practised routine; where I'm going next and how soon I'm going there. Actually I don't yet know where, but it's true I'll be gone soon. Decades will pass before I come back here. Once they know Dobbin the Dormobile is my permanent home, but their village isn't, my audience is on my side.

One says, "I have too many runner beans. You're welcome to pick a few."

"Are you OK for bedding? Only I've got a spare duvet that's just taking up space," someone else chips in.

The offer of things such as spare veg and household cast-offs isn't unusual. Sometimes it's motivated from kindness I'm sure, but also I suspect the hope that if I'm given what they don't mind me having, I won't decide to take anything else. I accept everything – if I don't need it I can usually sell or trade it.

"That's very kind, Mrs …?"

They give me their names and I tell them I'm Rose Boswell.

Now the introductions have been made I feel sure I'm going to achieve what I came here for. "Life on the road can be very hard sometimes," I say. "Any money I earn doesn't go far – not as far as I do." That gets a little laugh and a lot of sympathy.

Linda Jones says, "I have a set of camping pots, plates and cutlery. My daughter bought all sorts, but never used it before she … Well, if any of it's any use to you …"

Bingo! "That would be wonderful. All my stuff is really old and worn. Which is your house? I'll come and get it, save you carrying it out."

She hesitates about telling me and therefore practically inviting me into her home, but the runner bean lady gives me her own address adding, "Linda Jones lived right next door".

I pay for my cheese and a bottle of milk, which helps establish my honesty, then make arrangements to accept all their offers. I soon have a good supply of fresh vegetables and new-to-me pots and cutlery to cook and eat them with. I'm putting everything away when someone knocks on my door.

The woman, Sharon Blanchard, was the only one of those I'd met in the shop who hadn't offered me anything. She's come to suggest I might like to move the van.

I do get that, and sometimes abuse about thieving gypsies, but my reassuring spiel usually works. Sharon had heard that, and seemed to accept it, so I thought she'd be fairly happy for me to stick around a day or so.

"There's a level space right outside our house, just over there," she points. "It would be quieter and safer as it's not on the road …"

Ah, that was OK then. I looked out. "The one with the for sale sign?"

"Yes. If you like you could put a load in our washing machine, use the shower."

As you can imagine it's a tempting offer. Also a very surprising one. Few people invite me inside. Linda Jones asked me to share a pot of tea and some biscuits, but that was partly to assuage her guilt for being suspicious of me and partly because she was eager to talk. Sometimes it's easier to say things to a complete stranger than to confide in those who already know most of your business.

"Got people coming to view the house have you?" I guess that's Sharon's reason for being so helpful.

"Er, yes. Soon. And you… you are staying a few days?"

"Absolutely I am. Two at the most."

I move Dobbin, putting him right where she suggests. Further back amongst the trees would have been less conspicuous, but she's right that closer to the front gate is where it's most level.

She's insistent that I put clothes in the machine. When I bring them in and she's set it going she says, "I hope you're not offended, but I have some things I don't wear now. They'd be more suitable for someone your age."

I don't ask her what age she thinks that is. She'd guess wrong for sure. The clothes are bright, flowing and floral. They suggest she was a child of the sixties, but she seems too young. Maybe she wore them for a part in the village play, or to a fancy dress party – or some other occasion where she'd wanted to look like a gypsy?

They are pretty and good quality, so of course I accept.

"You could put them on, after your shower. Make sure they fit OK."

She's strangely insistent and I can think of no reason to refuse. I'm well enough used to manipulating others with reassuring words that I easily recognise the same tactic being used on me.

Once clean and dressed in the clothes she put out, we drink tea and she asks if I'll read her leaves.

I don't bother telling her that I'm not technically a gypsy as it seems clear she wants me to be one and it's so much easier to let people keep their assumptions than to tell the truth.

"You have a happy future, which you'll share with loved ones," I say. The many family photos make that seem likely. "There will be changes, but they'll bring improvements and... um, unexpected bonuses." I waffle on for a bit, saying the kind of things she probably wants to hear.

"Thank you. I hope you're right."

"You don't sound convinced."

"You're not an actual gypsy, are you?"

I admit it, but offer no details.

"Just for a moment I thought... but it might not matter. If you look like a gypsy and act like one, it could still work."

"I can tell you want something from me and from the way you keep checking your watch, it may be as well to tell me the whole story quickly. Then I'll see if it's something I'm prepared to do."

"In a way it's simple. There are people coming to view the house. I thought if they thought gypsies often camped in the area, it might put them off. Sorry, that's not a very pc thing to say, but ..."

"It's OK, " I assure her. Some travellers deserve their bad reputation and anyway they're not my problem. "So you want me to clear off now, so I don't put them off?"

"No, I want you to stay so you do."

"I can help put them off, but taking down the for sale sign might be a better option."

"It's not that simple. My husband …"

"Ah, he wants to sell, but you don't?"

"He doesn't either. The house has been in his family for generations. Trouble is there's a bakery business, which has been in my family even longer. It's struggling and he wants to sell the house to help keep it going. I'd rather we sold the business. If we do it now we'll still get enough for a comfortable retirement, the bakery would keep operating and our staff's jobs will be safe. That's all I'm really concerned about."

"Why not tell him that?"

"I have, but he doesn't quite believe me. Our relationship has always been a bit restrained, a bit polite."

"Oh?"

"I can see it's going to have to be the whole story with you. The truth is we had to get married. I was pregnant."

That doesn't sound massively restrained to me. It does show my guess about her age is probably right after all. If she'd got pregnant in the sixtes she'd have been expected to marry pdq and never mind the strain that put on the relationship.

"We've got on well enough, and had another child. Both are doing well in different areas. That's another reason we don't need to keep the business. But I think even now he doesn't realise how much I love him and I don't know exactly how he feels about me."

"Why is he selling the house which means so much to him?"

"Because he thinks it'll save something more important to me. My family's business," Sharon says.

"Then you have your answer. Doesn't take a gypsy to see that if he's putting you first, he must care about your happiness more than he does about his own wishes."

I see a warm glow from her as she realises I've spoken the truth. She hasn't though, not all of it.

"What's with the gypsy blouse and tea reading and stuff? I understand you wanted my van out there to scare off the first lot of people who're coming to view, but that would just be temporary. There's more to it than that."

"I want my husband to believe a gypsy is stopping us selling the house. It's a family legend that a gypsy has helped each time there's been a risk of that. I though that if he saw what looked like one, he'd be shocked into listening to, and believing, me."

"I'll play my part, but only if you agree to play yours and tell him the truth."

"I will, I promise."

Sharon must have stuck to it, because the 'For sale' sigh comes down before I'm ready to move on. I'm glad about that and that I'd helped the Blanchards realise how much they cared about each other, but not as pleased as I am to see Linda Jones' daughter arrive and the two of them hug. That was my real mission here – to bring them back together. Clearly the little chat Linda and I had when I collected the camping pots and plates has done the trick.

There's a tap on my door.

"Rose Boswell?" a postman asks.

I admit it and he hands me a very old looking letter, which I open eagerly. 'Destination Little Mallow' I read and think it's a mistake, until I see the name – Sharon Blanchard. I skim through the details, confirming that my 'new' mission is one I've already accomplished. Excellent!

As I'm ahead of schedule I can take a little holiday. I manoeuvre Dobbin the Dormobile out onto the road, being careful of the flower beds. It's a much easier task with a small campervan than with the big horse and heavy wooden caravan I had last time I parked here!

Think I'll head for the coast. I've not been back to Weymouth since the 30's when I persuaded a runaway child to swallow his pride and go back home. Too late to look in on him, but perhaps I can convince his great-grandson that a strange women in a campervan will make an interesting new friend. One he'd like to share his catch with. I do like a nice bit of fresh mackerel and it'd go smashing with all those runner beans.

22. Shanghaied

"Julie, do you have a minute?"

"Of course, Carla," Julie said.

It was already five thirty-five on Friday – Julie was partly disappointed to be delayed, but felt she'd had a lucky escape. If she'd left on time, come Monday she'd have faced Carla's wrath for not being available when wanted, despite the request not coming until after she should have left.

"As you may know, I'm considering appointing a deputy."

Julie nodded. There had been speculation in the office about when Carla would finally get around to making it official. Everyone knew George would get the post. He was the most senior, most qualified, and best able to cope with the indecisive, impulsive and frankly impossible Carla.

"Well?" Carla demanded. Clearly she felt she'd asked a question and expected an answer.

"I… " Julie hoped that as well as being supremely organised, immensely tactful and incredibly flexible, poor George was also a mindreader. Those skills would all be required in his new role.

"There's a great deal of prestige attached, travel opportunities, the possibility of taking over from me when I join the board."

"Of course," Julie murmured, both to show she understood what was required of the new deputy and that she didn't doubt Carla would rise further still. Wasn't there a saying about promoting people until they reached a level where they could do no harm?

"Obviously there would be an increase in salary. Fifteen percent."

Julie couldn't help wondering why they were having this conversation. Discretion wasn't one of Carla's strong points, but even so discussing a colleague's pay seemed odd.

"It's a good opportunity," Carla insisted.

"Yes. I'm sure George will… "

"George?"

"Aren't you going to offer him the job?" she asked hoping that for once Carla would give a clear answer.

"The man's an idiot."

OK, that was pretty clear. In that case, who was she going to choose? Oh! The rest of the conversation now made sense – Carla wanted Julie as her deputy! Could she really mean that? "Do you mean you want me …?"

"Why do you think we're having this conversation?" Carla interrupted.

"I'll need time to think about it," Julie managed to say.

"Good grief! This all needs to be put in place before the Shanghai operation starts."

That was less than two weeks! That was absolutely typical of the woman. She could have taken on a deputy months ago, and been around to show them what was expected, before she flew out. Or at least what was expected at the time of instruction; no doubt it would change the moment they got the hang of things.

Julie only said she needed time because she couldn't immediately think of a way to refuse which wouldn't damage her career. Working directly under Carla would be a nightmare. But when she got home that evening and mentioned it to her flatmate, Lynnette asked if she was going to accept.

"No way! Carla is a pain to work for. She never properly explains anything, she's indecisive… "

"At the moment, but wouldn't things be different for her deputy? They'd need to know exactly what was going on."

"I suppose so. It was her own idea to have a deputy, so she must see the need for someone to be totally in her confidence. And when she's absent, as she will be quite often once the Shanghai thing starts, they would be able to act for her, so could take the decisions she didn't get around to."

"Precisely. And you've been hoping for promotion, haven't you?"

Julie admitted it.

"Is the money better?" Lynnette asked.

"Much."

"There you go then."

Julie thought it over during the weekend. It really was a great opportunity. The only snag was Carla herself, and Julie would still have to work with her some of the time, whether or not she accepted. Maybe she'd see less of her? Carla mentioned travel, so maybe Julie would sometimes be the one working away, while Carla remained in the office? She'd love to fly out to Shanghai, or any of the other locations where the company conducted business. And the extra pay would make a huge difference.

"Carla, do you have a minute?" Julie asked first thing Monday.

"Sorry, no. Can't George help?"

"George?"

"Yes, I've just appointed him as my deputy."

"But you offered that post to me!"

"No I didn't. I asked what you thought about it. George was taking so long to accept and asking for so many assurances in writing I thought he might be silly and say no. You convinced me he just needed time to think it over."

"But…"

"Actually, I did briefly consider offering it to you, but you're so indecisive and half the time I don't think you really understand what I'm saying." Carla strode off, leaving Julie partly feeling disappointed, but mostly relieved she'd had a very lucky escape.

23. Wonderful Dream

You know those stories where the person wakes up and it was all a wonderful dream? Well, that's exactly what I'm hoping is going on here. I'm floating in the night sky, totally alone, suspended by cords from a huge nylon mushroom. Given the fact I've never been what you'd call adventurous, and I've been paralysed from the neck down since birth, does that seem likely to be real to you? And it's normal to dream, isn't it?

As well as the parachute harness, I'm wearing my pyjamas, which would seem to support the dream theory. Although I don't remember a jump or even a push, I know, in the way you do know things in dreams, that I started off in a plane and that there was nothing wrong with it. I very much doubt that even those who regularly jump out of perfectly good aircraft do so in their sleep. And even those who'd feel comfortable doing the school run in their dressing gown probably consider sky diving enough of an event to get dressed for.

Generally I'm not good with heights – and for me, having my head six foot above the ground would feel really high. I'm way above that! Above the tallest of people, trees, buildings. I'm almost up with the clouds. From up here the street lights, headlights and houselights are just a faint glow. A glow that's receding. I flail my arms and legs in panic.

It really is a dream then. It has to be. I can only move unaided in my electric chair, and in my dreams. To start with this nocturnal fantasy is not so wonderful. Then I drift higher and higher, through soft cushions of cumulus. Or is it cirrus? Whatever it is, it's damp, but in a surprisingly pleasant way. Refreshing, cleansing, and not soaking through my PJs.

Then the clouds clear and I'm surrounded by starlight. Galaxies swirl into spirals like the cinnamon layer in the pinwheel biscuits Granny used to make. The colours though are different. Oh, those colours! Pinks, purples and metallic blue, radiating out into the darkness. Distant stars twinkle bright white and gold, like a child's laughter. I meander through constellations whose patterns seem familiar. Mythical beasts and familiar creatures, chased to the heavens by Greek gods and legendary heroes. I drift up and up and up, never worrying about the coming down. Not now that I'm sure it's a dream. Of course I'll wake and crash to Earth – but I'll wake safe with my head on my soft pillow, and warm duvet tucked under my chin.

At last I do come down. Gently. Like a downy feather slowly see-sawing towards the earth. Like a petal from a fading flower. Like a single tear. The ground doesn't rush up to meet me, but waits patiently for me to land. I wake before that happens. I'm not relieved it's over, nor disappointed for the same reason. I'll experience one of those emotions tomorrow. Maybe both.

No, not tomorrow. It's morning now. My parachute jump, a real one, my first one, will happen today. I'm excited, nervous but not yet scared.

No doubt there will be some anxiety as well as anticipation when I'm in the plane, waiting to leave. I expect to feel some fear as well as freedom when I first leave that safety. I shouldn't be frightened, not really. For one thing I won't be alone, but strapped to an experienced professional. Just as in the dream I won't recall the jump from the plane. That's because there won't be any jump – it's just a small step I've been told. That's the instructor's job. He'll make the decisions, take the actions. I'll just be a passenger, enjoying the view.

It will be daylight. Clear and bright, or we're not going. And we won't be drifting up, even though it will look and feel that way the moment the cord is pulled and the canopy expands. We'll descend fast, but not too fast, and land gently I hope, the instructor and I.

And I won't flail my arms and legs in panic. Not as we wait to go, not as we leave the plane. Not as the ground below stops looking like a map and becomes real and ever closer. Not ever. Unlike when I slept in my pyjamas and drifted through the starry sky, I'll still be paralysed.

But just for a little while that won't matter at all. Amongst those jumping for the first time, I'll be the same as everyone else. And that really will be a wonderful dream come true.

24. Awkward Encounter

Macey spotted Duncan on the crowded high street. He was hard to miss being so broad shouldered, tall and attractive. Macey, short, slim and honey blonde was more easily overlooked. She considered hiding out in a shop, to avoid the heartache and embarrassment if he wasn't pleased to see her. But supposing he saw her do that and thought she didn't want to speak to him? Or he would have been happy to stop and chat and she missed the opportunity? They needed to talk and Macey needed to be brave.

She waved, and to her relief Duncan waved back. Not the polite acknowledgement of a long time acquaintance he couldn't easily avoid, but the grinning, pleased to see her salute he'd always given in such situations.

After last week, after what she'd done, she'd wondered if that would still be the case. Worried it wouldn't. He'd come into her life as her brother's friend. Over time he'd become hers too. It was a huge relief to know she hadn't ruined that.

As he made his way purposefully towards her, Duncan continued to smile at Macey, and even to occasionally wave, as though to emphasis the fact he was on his way towards her. He disrupted the flow of foot traffic. Men moved around him giving way to something more than themselves, as though he were a rock in the stream. Duncan's presence was even more disruptive to women.

They either instinctively moved a little closer, or drew back to get a better look.

Why should Macey behave differently? He was worth looking at. Macey had been casting glances at Duncan for some time now. Years in fact. She was sure he'd known when they were younger that she'd had a crush on him, but he'd continued to treat her just the same. He was kind, sweet and it seemed was always a part of her life.

He raised his hand and grinned again. She smiled back and waved again. He was still some distance away. They'd either have to repeat that several times, or ignore each other until he reached her side. This was a classically awkward situation, but nothing to how strained their relationship had been since last week's end of summer beach party.

It had been their usual crowd. Her brother and his friends, Macey and hers. They'd had a barbecue, with plenty of food and a little sweet cider. There had been laughter, games and dancing – a lot of each of those. The evening was exceptionally warm for early autumn and most people stayed late.

Macey must have fallen asleep, because she woke to hear Duncan saying, "Come on, sleepy head," and feel him gently shake her shoulder.

Telling herself she was dreaming, Macey had kissed him. Not just the peck on the cheek she'd given him occasionally before, whenever she could pretend the situation warranted it, but a proper kiss. At first he'd responded and it had been glorious. Both the kiss itself, and the hope he felt about her as she did about him, were wonderful. Then he'd stopped and moved away.

"The tide is coming in," he said. "We have to go."

Waves were indeed lapping against the ash of the fire on which they'd cooked their food a few hours earlier. Macey tried to stand. Either she was still a little sleepy, or the kiss had made her legs unable to support her. Either way, she found herself stumble against Duncan.

"Need help?" he asked

When she nodded he scooped her into his arms. He carried her up the beach, with the sunset lighting the sky and reflecting in his eyes like a scene from a romantic film.

"Thanks for saving me," she'd said. There hadn't been any real danger of her drowning, but she might easily have got cold and wet before waking.

For a moment she thought he'd kiss her, or at least say something, but he just touched her cheek briefly, shook his head and turned away. She felt so many emotions swirl through her as he strode along the shore. The were joined by a touch of relief when she realised he wasn't leaving altogether, but had gone to help her brother gather their litter and double check they'd not left any burning embers.

Over the next few days Duncan had almost ignored her. He wasn't rude, and didn't avoid coming to the house or joining in things Macey and her brother did together, but he was just one of the crowd. Only then did she realise they'd become more than that. He'd not just been her brother's friend, but hers too. Had she lost that, just because she couldn't resist kissing him? Or was it just their embarrassment afterwards causing the trouble?

"Macey," Duncan said when he at last reached her.

"Hi."

They were close enough to touch, to share their customary hug, but didn't. Macey wanted to reach for him, but daren't. She wasn't sure she could hold him briefly. The holding part would be no trouble, but letting go immediately afterwards would be impossible.

Something held Duncan back too. "Well, this is awkward," he said, putting her thoughts into words.

Macey had to fix this. Must admit her mistake, so they could put it behind them. "Sorry. It's my fault."

"Yours?"

"The beach party... when I kissed you... "

"Macey," he murmured. He'd not been standing at much of a distance, but moved closer. "You didn't kiss me. I kissed you."

She was going to deny it, but tilted her head to look up at him and wasn't sure. When he woke her, his lips would have been way above hers, wouldn't they? He'd easily have been able to avoid a kiss if it hadn't been welcome.

"I didn't kiss you?" she asked.

"No."

"Well I should have." She stood on the tips of her toes and did just that.

Duncan responded and it was glorious.

Thank you for reading this book. I hope you enjoyed it. If you did, I'd really appreciate it if you could leave a short review on Amazon and/or Goodreads.

To learn more about my writing life, hear about new releases and get a free short story, sign up to my newsletter – https://mailchi.mp/677f65e1ee8f/sign-up or you can find the link on my website patsycollins.uk

More Books by Patsy Collins

Novels

Firestarter
Escape To The Country
A Year And A Day
Paint Me A Picture
Leave Nothing But Footprints
Acting Like A Killer

Non-fiction –

From Story Idea To Reader
(co-written with Rosemary J. Kind)

A Year Of Ideas:
365 sets of writing prompts and exercises

Short story collections –

Over The Garden Fence
Up The Garden Path
Through The Garden Gate
In The Garden Air

No Family Secrets
Can't Choose Your Family
Keep It In The Family
Family Feeling
Happy Families

All That Love Stuff
With Love And Kisses
Lots Of Love
Love Is The Answer

Slightly Spooky Stories I
Slightly Spooky Stories II
Slightly Spooky Stories III
Slightly Spooky Stories IV

Just A Job
Perfect Timing
A Way With Words
Dressed To Impress
Coffee & Cake
Not A Drop To Drink
Criminal Intent

Printed in Great Britain
by Amazon